COUNTING MY BUTTONS

COUNTING MY BUTTONS

by

ESTHER PENCE GARBER

The Brethren Press, Elgin, Illinois

COUNTING MY BUTTONS

Copyright © 1979, by the Brethren Press, Elgin, Ill.

Printed in the United States of America

Cover Design by Wendell Mathews

Library of Congress Cataloging in Publication Data

Garber, Esther Pence, 1910-
Counting my buttons.

1. Garber, Esther Pence, 1910- , in fiction, drama, poetry, etc. I. Title.
PZ4.G2137Co]PS3557.A6[813'.5'4 79-544
ISBN 0-87178-157-3

Published by the Brethren Press, Elgin, Ill.

Distributed by Two Continents Publishing Group, LTD.
171 Madison Avenue, New York, N.Y. 10016

To all children who dream dreams—
and in particular to Mark, Erik, and Lie,
my grandchildren.

Rich man, poor man,
Beggar man, thief,
Doctor, lawyer,
Indian chief.

Housewife, teacher,
Missionary afar,
Nurse, "glad girl,"
Movie star.

What shall I be?

CONTENTS

PREFACE

Upon concluding the final chapter of my little book *Button Shoes*, I felt a sense of satisfaction in having completed a project that I had looked forward to for a number of years. I thought the full story of my ''growing up years'' had been told. But in the passage of time I began to sense that this was not true—as the days went by I again uncovered hidden and almost forgotten incidents in my memory and those of my living brother and sisters and friends. Stories of a living breathing family of eleven children and a Mother and Pappy who watched over them. A family learning to live together, to work and play together, to cooperate, to disagree, and yes, to sometimes spat and quarrel and fight. It is the story of a family that experienced joy and sadness, hardships and pleasures, laughter and tears, successes and failures.

It is also the story of a girl who dreamed of what she would someday be as a grownup—a movie star, a missionary, a ''glad girl''—and how at last she was awakening to her first tiny concept of the real meaning of ''being.''

Many more events will never be told because they cannot be recalled. One is not privileged to remember the whole of one's past, only bits and pieces, vignettes, sometimes pictures without words that flash before the mind's eye.

As was said in *Button Shoes*, and can be said again, most of the events or happenings contained herein are true or could have been true. Any embellishments or fictional aspects are designed to make it come alive for the reader. And again, times, dates, names and chronological order may not be totally correct; it was not my purpose to make them so. I relied mostly on memories which were not always reliable. Certain activities and events have been mentioned with little detail, inasmuch as rather complete descriptions were given in *Button Shoes*.

One finds the help of others quite valuable in the pursuit of any project, so I want to say, ''Danke schee'' for reading and correcting, and especially for encouraging, to my friend and neighbor Virginia Andes, my niece Pat Showalter, and to Bill, my own special Dutchman. A ''Danke'' also to Janet Earhart for an excellent job in typing the manuscript. And finally, my appreciation to the Mill Creek and Bridgewater Churches of the Brethren for affording me access to the minutes of The Sisters' Aid Societies, dating back to the year 1899.

If *Button Shoes* brought you any pleasure or gave you any new insights about earlier times, perhaps *Counting My Buttons* can help you reflect a bit more and bring a few more hours of reading enjoyment.

MEET THE PENCE FAMILY

If you did not come to know my family in *Button Shoes*, I want to introduce them to you now:

PAPPY—Life became meaningful for me at about the age of three when I became aware that I had a rugged six foot father (Pappy) with white hair, a full white beard, and eyes as blue as the sky on a clear day. His face was patterned with lines—good lines, beautiful lines, etched there by the sun, the wind, the cold of our valley. There were smile and laughter lines too, engraved by the effervescence and aliveness of a brood of eleven living children.

And there was **MOTHER**—short, fat, rotund and so typically Dutch. Her hair was parted in the middle and combed around to be caught in a bun at the back of her head, exposing a gentle face dominated by large hazel eyes. Pappy said that when she was young she was the prettiest girl in the neighborhood, and always added, ''She still is.'' Who could possible disagree?

Then there was **LIZZIE FLORA**, the first born. By the time I was three and old enough to be aware of people and places, Lizzie had gone out into the world to pursue her chosen profession, teaching in public school. My memories of her were formed on weekends and summers when she came home to be with her family. We were always glad to have her back among us to talk about her work and to help at the farm. Lizzie, later Elizabeth, was pretty and proud—too proud to be called the undignified name of ''Lizzie.''

GRACE ARLENE—Grace possessed what young farm girls can only dream about. She was already married to a handsome dentist, had a home in the big city of Baltimore, and had been to places and had seen things that we could not envision even in our dreams. So Grace, too, was rather on the periphery of my farm experiences.

JASPER HARSHBARGER—Jasper was always the quiet thoughtful one, grown up beyond his years, taking on responsibilities at an early age. Perhaps, the rugged and vigorous farm life of those early times often demanded that, especially of the eldest in the family. He had stopped going to school in his early teens to become Pappy's right hand man on the farm and, besides, he never seemed to enjoy school anyhow.

Then came **CHARLES JOSEPH**—Charlie was born full of merriment and foolishness mixed with not a small amount of deviltry. He often kept us in stitches with his humor and puckish tricks. Even as he grew older, he never took life very seriously, and went out into the world at a rather early age to seek his fortune. But home seemed to pull him back often for many visits with us, to the delight of all.

And **BERTHA OLA**—Bertha and Charlie were not twins, but at least they must have been born under the same sign of the Zodiac, for she, too, was high-spirited and full of mirth. Between the two of them, they kept things rather lively around the farm. As Bertha matured, however, she displayed a serious nature as well, and Mother depended on her often to help supervise and guide her younger brothers and sisters. Later, she pursued her chosen career with vigor and determination. She, too, became a school teacher.

RUTH MAGDALENE—By this time, some one must have decided that Mother and Pappy needed a break, a respite from the high-spirits of the former two, for Ruth was gentle, sweet and modest. In fact, a bit more than modest, she was somewhat shy, so that she blushed at almost any provocation. The blush made her even more beautiful on the outside, but less comfortable on the inside.

MARY HOPE—I wonder why there is one in every family that the rest like to tease? In ours it was Mary. As she grew up, however, she took her rightful place beside us, and sometimes against us. She loved pretty clothes and she generally managed to get whatever her older sisters, Elizabeth, Bertha and Ruth acquired, whether it was a new dress or a pair of laced, white high-top shoes.

WILBUR SAMUEL and **JACOB DAVID**—They were typical prepuberty boys—obstreperous, bullyish, pesky, contrary, and "lubbardy" (clumsy)—what other adjectives do you apply to boys of that age? They loved to tease their two little sisters, and I guess we sometimes loved it too. Isn't it strange how one feels disgust and love at the same time for members of his own family? That sums up how we all felt about our two young brothers.

JAMES HAROLD—Born January 14, 1909; died June 30, 1909.

ESTHER VIRGINIA—What about me? I'll assign to you the prerogative to form your own judgment and characterization of me as you read my story.

At last, **FRANCES ELLEN**—She was the happy, placid,

curly-headed baby of our family. She mostly liked to sit around, laugh and gurgle, and grow fat. She would enter into activities with me after a little urging and prodding. We were not far apart in age so we spent many happy childhood hours together.

PART ONE: THE YEAR OF MARY PICKFORD

To Town and Back

Rich man, poor man,
Beggar man, thief,
Doctor, lawyer,
Indian chief!

"Turn around, Frances, let me count your buttons so we can find out what you're gonna' be when you grow up," I suggested.

Frances turned, and as I touched each button on the back of her dress I started counting, "Rich man, poor man, beggar man, thief. . . . aw, Frances, you're gonna' be a thief. Shame on you!"

"I'm not gonna' be a thief either," Frances countered. "Hey, I have a button on the side of my drawers you didn't count, so that makes me a doctor," she supplied, doing a bit of fast thinking.

"Ha! Ha! Ha! Frances a doctor," laughed Wilbur. "Whoever heard of a girl doctor? If you wanna' know whose gonna' really be somebody important, I'll count my buttons," he said. "Rich man, poor man, beggar man, thief, doctor, lawyer, . . . just what I'd planned."

"Wilbur, you counted one that has popped off; that's not fair!" I scolded.

"I can't help it if the button's gone. Turn around and let me do yours, Esther."

I turned and Wilbur started counting, "Rich man, poor man, . . . that's all the buttons you have left on your dress. You're gonna' be a poor man."

"Yeah, Esther's gonna' be a poor man! Esther's gonna' be a poor man!" mimicked Jake.

"How can I be a poor man when I'm not a man?" I argued. "Anyway, Wilbur cheated me, I don't have but one button on the back of my dress. The girls must'a rubbed the others off on the washboard. So if I don't have but one button I'll be a rich man."

"Huh!" Wilbur countered. "If you're not a man and can't be a poor man, then you can't be a rich man either."

"Don't either one of you make no sense," interrupted Jake. "I got all my buttons; come and count mine."

So down his shirt I went, "Rich man, poor man, beggar man, thief, doctor, lawyer, Indian chief."

"Just what I'd like to be when I grow up, an Indian chief!" Jake exclaimed happily.

"How in the world can you be an Indian chief when you're not an Indian?" I asked.

" 'Bout the only Indian he'd ever make would be a cigar store Indian," laughed Wilbur.

Just then Mother called from the kitchen door, "Come on in, children, dinner's ready."

We dashed across the porch and into the kitchen to be the first to the tin wash pan which sat in its customary spot, the iron sink behind the kitchen door. After our slap-dash washing was over, we searched for the dry spots on the towel that were never quite there.

The older girls, Elizabeth, Bertha and Ruth, were helping Mother get dinner on the table. As they took the lid off the iron pot filled with new beans and potatoes, the steam and the good smell permeated the kitchen, tempting our appetites. The girls quickly dipped the vegetables into the dishes and placed them on our long family table; the onions sliced in vinegar were already there. When it came to eating beans we all had an onion habit, with no worries about odor or the need for a breath deodorant (product unknown). We all ate them, thus we were not obnoxious to each other, and seldom were there social functions to attend—and who was Emily Post? This was perfect freedom to eat that which we enjoyed.

A plate of homemade bread and a sort of shapeless blob of homemade butter that had been dipped into over and over as it made its rounds, were at their respective places. Additionally there was that inexorable bowl of deep red apple butter, for me the spread of last resort. I often thought when Mother or Pappy cautioned us not to waste any food and to "remember the starving Armenians," I would gladly have donated them the last crock of it stored on the wash house loft, plus that thick smelly bowl on the table.

By this time the men, Pappy, Charlie and Jasper, and the would-be men, Wilbur and Jake, had come in from the field at the correct time. It seems that farmers have a built-in time clock, especially when it's meal time. In short order, every one had scrambled to his or her place at the table: Pappy at the head, the boys to his right in chronological order, Mother to his left, the older girls along the table beside her, also in chronological order—Frances and I on a small made-for-two bench down at the end of the table, opposite our Pappy.

After we had settled down to eating dinner and small talking in between mouthfuls, Pappy interrupted the chatter to inform us, "Your Mother and I plan to go to Harrisonburg on Monday since it's Court Day. We have lots of longstem apples on hand now so we thought we might take some along to sell; they go pretty good."

All eyes looked up expectantly—or hopefully.

Mother added, "Now don't any of you older ones get your hopes up about going along. We thought it was time for Esther and Frances to go. It's only fair that they get to see what a city is like too."

Wilbur butted in, "Gee whiz! Those two babies? A horse and buggy might run over them! There's even some cars on the streets now!"

Jake, always following his slightly older brother's ideas, chimed in, "Yeah, and they are such babies, they are liable to get lost!"

Not appreciating such inferences, and letting no time pass without a retort, I shouted, "Don't talk about us! How about you all when you went to town and sneaked off, and Jake fell in the 'crick' by the Junk Yard and got his clothes all wet?"

This retort was accompanied by a snoot at my two brothers, and Frances, ever my mimic, did likewise.

They returned the compliment with snoots at us, but Jake, trying to get by with a little deception, exclaimed, "Mother. Esther and Frances made snoots at us!"

Frances and I in self-defensive unison retorted, "You did too! You made snoots at us!"

At this point Pappy took over clearly and firmly, stating, "Any more of this fussing and you four will leave the table. Now let's get busy and finish your dinners."

As Pappy and Mother resumed their eating, I made one final "so there" snoot at my brothers.

Wilbur yelled, "Pappy, Esther did it again!"

The last words: "Wilbur, you and Esther leave the table."

In time, when Wilbur and Jake reconciled themselves to the certainty that they were not going to town on Monday rather than Frances and me, their attitude shifted to one of worldly wisdom. They volunteered to tell us how to behave in the big city: how not to get lost—how not to get run over—how not to get robbed. Robbed of what, I wondered.

"Now, girls, eat your breakfasts or you'll get hungry later on. We'll be in Harrisonburg over dinner time," Mother advised.

My inner response to this suggestion was, "I don't want anything to eat; let's get goin'." Excitement had filled my stomach to capacity. However, I wisely allowed that thought to remain inside, but I slyly tried to give the appearance of eating. I slowly crumbled a small piece of bread all over my plate and dribbled a spoon of flour gravy over this, trying to disguise my small helping. When the dish of stewed apples was passed I again made an effort to be deceptive in the amount I served myself, dipping in the dish two or three times but taking only one schnitz (piece) on each dip. Swallowing wasn't easy, but swallow it I did, before anyone reminded me to clean up my plate and to remember the starving Armenians.

In our family, when one reached the approximate age of eight there was a certain absoluteness about washing and wiping the dishes, as if it were preordained. So by now this chore was a regular for Frances and me.

On this particular morning I suspect that Frances and I set a Pence record for the least amount of time consumed in washing and drying the dishes—perhaps no record was set for thoroughness.

Not by choice, but because it was our Mother's instruction, we pumped a foot tub of water from the cistern and scrubbed our feet and legs, then washed our faces and hands in the pan at the kitchen sick (our weekly baths having been taken on the preceding Saturday). We scrambled into our Sunday dresses and dashed down the stairs where Ruth was waiting to comb our "stroobly" hair. She completed the job by fastening a big ribbon bow on the top of each of our heads.

By now Pappy and Mother were in their Sunday outfits. Mother's dark dress extended from her neck to her ankles, with just the toes of her plain black laced-up shoes peeping out. There was a bit of lace at the neck of her dress to give a soft touch to her lovely serene face. She placed her black bonnet over her hair, which was neatly brushed to a tuck at the back of her head, and tied it securely under her chin.

The style of Pappy's clothes never changed; there were always the long black trousers covering his long legs and always ending at his plain black shoes. The same plain black coat buttoned all the way to his neck where it could no longer take cover under a white beard, for he had recently reduced his full blown beard to a remnant of its former size. Protruding above the narrow banded coat collar was a rigid white celluloid collar that seemed to be an essential part of the Brethren's plain clothes. Whoever created that style must have believed that "man was made to suffer all his days." And whenever I happened to notice that part of Pappy's outfit, I thought, "That's enough to make one glad to be a girl."

By this time the boys had tied the horse to the hitching post near the gate.

Pappy hadn't yet learned to drive our new Maxwell car, and for some reason he never did. Although he could handle a team of horses hitched to any farm vehicle, he could never get the hang of driving that "cantankerous, obstinate, sputtering, onery" collection of nuts, bolts, cloth and metal, capable of being held together with a piece of bailing wire.

So began a treat for two young farm girls who had seldom been outside the orbit of church, school and friend's homes. The trip was a long buggy ride to Harrisonburg, a long ten miles away. Up and down the dusty roads we went, moving sometimes at a walk and sometimes at a trot: past our white wooden school with its windows shuttered for the summer and its inevitable bell tower; past the little Methodist Church nearby snuggling under its assortment of trees; on to Keezletown Road where Pappy "geed" Chester, the horse, to the right with a slight tug of the line in his right hand; past tidy farm buildings with their rolling fields surrounding them; past Yager's Store where we always purchased my much despised school shoes; then on to the Cross Roads and the Spotswood Trail where Pappy "hawed" Chester to the left this time and pointed him in the direction of Harrisonburg several miles away.

From that moment on, the time and distance seemed endless to Frances and me. As we approached town, the Spotswood Trail disappeared into East Market Street.

Our first stop was at the market where farmers bought and sold horses, not that Pappy had any for sale or was anticipating the buying of one. However, he reckoned correctly that it would be a logical place to sell the sack of apples that he had brought with us, since it was probable that many men would be congregating there for their horse trading. He soon disposed of the apples and could have sold more had there been room in our buggy to bring them along. I suspect he preferred to have his two daughters accompany him rather than a hard knobby sack of apples. The air was already heavy with dust kicked up by the prancing feet of horses and the movement of the crowd. The farmers strode about slapping the sides of the horses, inspecting their teeth to determine age, and looking them over fore and aft with a practiced eye. And all the while scratching their heads trying to figure out how to strike a bargain.

I was still fascinated at the skill with which they spat their amber juice from their mouths in the most convenient direction and at such great distances, but Mother concluded this was not a proper place for bonnets and skirts so we left as soon as Pappy's transaction was completed.

If one were a stranger travelling through the Shenandoah Valley at the present time, the appearance of buggies, surreys, spring wagons and buckboards might seem quaint. But as we drove on down East Market Street near Court Square, we did not appear at all out of place, for even though there was a patch work of cars and horse drawn vehicles, we buggy people were still in the majority.

Pappy found a place to park his rig. Frances and I quickly jumped down from the buggy, but Pappy and Mother were more sedate in their descent. After unhitching Chester, Pappy led him to a livery stable where he would remain until time to make the journey home.

As we walked to Court Square we saw tall buildings two, three, four, five, six stories high—rubbing shoulders and extending north, south, east and west. The big stone court house on the square in the midst was surrounded by an apron of green grass.

At this point we continued on past the Court House to the First National Bank where Pappy took care of his limited amount of banking. Inside were marble floors, hardwood tables, and cages with people inside. I stood spellbound by the sights and activity around me until Mother tugged my arm and said, "Esther, Pappy is through with his business and we must be going."

Outside again and we entered the hustle and bustle on the Square. People, mostly men, stood around in groups or milled around looking for a group to join. Pappy moved toward a knot of men dressed in the same black garb as himself; listened, and then entered the conversation. Pappy was never one to remain silent when current or mutual topics of interest were discussed.

"There sure is a big crowd in town today."

"Ja," responded a brother whose speech was still a kaleidoscope of both English and Dutch words. "Sure be; I had to leave my buckboard on German Street."

"Brother Kline, have you forgotten they don't call it German Street anymore? We are supposed to say Liberty Street now."

"Ja, I know, but I call it German Street yet still."

"I go along with Brother Kline. What right did they have to do that anyway? German Street is a good and fittin' name with so many German people living in Rockingham County."

"That's right! And what was their reason for changing the name? It's plain they did it out of hatred for the German people and the Kaiser because of the war."

"That's exactly right. They wanted to get the German name out of the area. I don't think God would approve of our holding grudges against anyone."

"Amen!"

Since gender was the determinant in those days as to who would stand and gossip around Court Square, Mother, Frances and I moved across the street to Lineweaver's Store where Pappy would join us for lunch. After having absorbed all the news and politics of the countryside, he arrived; but before joining us at the back of the store he stopped and purchased a hunk of aged yellow cheese that Mr. Lineweaver chopped from a large round cake, approximating the poundage that Pappy wanted. After paying for this, along with a poke of crackers, we sat down in the back of the store to have our lunch together. That cheese and those crackers tasted so good! We sometimes made 'schmierkees' (cottage cheese today) but the store-bought kind was something of a rarity with us. Those simple pleasures of a simpler time were indeed among the best.

Mother and Pappy still had some buying to do, thus after we had combed the crumbs from our laps so as not to waste a tiny bit, we climbed the gradual incline to B. Ney's Store.

When one lives in a time when styles are not constantly changing and one's manner of dress remains the same as my Pappy's and all the plain people's did, then clothes can be used until they are worn out. But now the time had come for Pappy to buy a new suit. B. Ney's Department Store was the one that stocked the clothes for the Brethren and Mennonites.

Mother also hoped to make a purchase, for Neys had run an advertisement in "The Daily News-Record" of a sale of some summer goods at twenty-one cents a yard. She decided to buy a few pieces to make dresses for the older girls and perhaps even Frances and me.

The patriarch, Mr. B. Ney, smoking a fat brown cigar stub moored between his lips, greeted his customers at the door with a solicitous "good day" and ushered them to whichever one of his sons could take care of their needs.

B. Ney's was the biggest store that Frances and I had ever been in, tables of dry goods and notions, racks of clothing, and rows upon rows of shoes in boxes all the way to the ceiling.

Pappy went to the men's ready-to-wear department for his suit of clothing, while Mother began scrutinizing the dress goods with the willing assistance of Frances and me.

"I like this pretty pink flowered piece."

"I like the blue one better. Blue is my favorite color. I look good in blue. That's what Elizabeth told me."

"Esther, you think too much about your looks. I don't know how you got to be so proud."

"That brown piece is ugly. I wouldn't want a dress made out of that. I would like to have this purple piece."

"That's not a very good piece," Mother said as she rubbed it, assessing its quality with practiced fingers. Mother loved beauty, too, but sometimes this had to give way to practicality when one nurtured and clothed a family of eleven children. After taking into consideration quality, beauty, and suggestions from Frances and me, the choices were made. The clerk measured and cut the specified amounts, then completed the transaction by folding the material in a piece of wrapping paper pulled from a roller with a cutting knife. He then tied it with a string unwound from a big spool that held yards and yards of white wrapping thread.

Now that all transactions were completed, Pappy said, "I think it's time that we get on the way."

Mother quickly agreed, then added, "I think while you get Chester hitched up I'll take Esther and Frances on down the street a ways so they can look around a little bit more."

Our sightseeing walk took us by Miller's Shoe Store, The Venda, an early version of a five and ten cent store, The Valley National Bank, Friddle's Restaurant, Yager's Shoe Store and the New Virginia Theatre.

By now Mother had decided it was time to turn and go back as Pappy was probably ready, but something caught my eye that challenged her intentions. The marquee at the theatre, in large bold letters read: "Now Playing, Mary Pickford in, 'Rebecca of Sunnybrook Farm.' "

"Mother! Mother! Look!" I shouted. "Look at the show they are havin'! I just finished readin' that book! Can't we go in to see it?"

"Not today, Esther, the show has already started, and anyhow, we have to be getting on our way home. Maybe if they show it for a day or so the older girls will want to see it and maybe they will let you go along."

"Oh, I sure hope so! Look at Mary Pickford! Isn't she beautiful?"

On one side of the big front doors were scenes from "Rebecca of Sunnybrook Farm":

Rebecca and Aunt Miranda
Rebecca and Aunt Jane
Rebecca and her friend, Emma Jane Perkins
But best of all there she was with
Adam Ladd!

On the opposite side of the doors was Miss Pickford in the rapturous embraces of Ramon Navarro, scenes from one of her earlier performances. I stood hypnotized, trying to absorb every detail of the scenes before me, until Mother took me by the arm and stated with emphasis, "Come on, Esther, we have to go now."

On the long return trip Frances was not much company, for we had not been long on the way when she fell asleep. Pappy was intent on covering the miles ahead and Mother in trying to keep Frances, who was as relaxed as a sack of flour, from falling out of the buggy. I was perfectly content at this turn of events, for I was left to pursue my reveries as the afternoon droned on. About the only sounds to be heard were the squeaking of the buggy shafts in rhythm to Chester's muted clops as they rose and fell in the thick dust of the road. There was an occasional "giddap" as Pappy tried to move Chester along a little faster. The now and then quiet bits of conversation that passed between Mother and Pappy went unnoticed by Frances and me.

This routine continued until Pappy turned off the Spotswood Trail and onto the Keezletown Road and headed in the direction of Cross Keys. Suddenly the right rear wheel of the buggy dropped into a deep rut, jolting Frances from her sleep and me from my reverie.

Frances sat up with a start, opened her eyes and asked, "Where are we?"

Pappy answered, "We are going towards Cross Keys."

Since we were now both awake and the name Cross Keys appropriately suggested to Pappy that this might be a good time and place for a history lesson, he quizzed, "Daughters, did you know that some of the Civil War was fought right here on this ground that we are now riding over?" He continued, "It was called the Battle of Cross Keys and Port Republic. General Stonewall Jackson was the leader of the Confederate Army."

"Were you born then, Pappy, and do you remember about it?" I asked.

"Yes, I was born in 1859, but I was too young to remember much about it. Yet I do recollect a few incidents."

"Tell us about it, Pappy," I begged.

And Frances added, "I want to hear about it too."

"Let me see now what I can remember," he began. "I was four years old when the battle of Gettysburg took place. The fighting was so fierce that when we put our ears to the ground we could hear the rumbling of the cannon fire all the way from there to here. I remember well hearing that."

"What else do you remember, Pappy? Tell us more," we begged.

"Well let's see now—I remember when General Sheridan and his men came through the Valley and burned most of the barns. They came to our place. Each morning my pa would take the cows and the horses up one of the hollows to hide them, so when the soldiers did come and burned our barn we saved our livestock. But they destroyed all the hay and grain in the barn. That was a very bad time for all the farmers around here, for even if they did save some of their stock, they didn't have much feed for them."

"That war was awful, wasn't it, Pappy?" Frances asked.

"Yes, daughter, very, very bad. All wars are bad. Maybe some day you can live in a world where there will be no more war and people can live at peace. That's why President Wilson is working so hard to form a league of nations."

After a short pause, Mother suggested, "They might like to hear the story about Grandma."

"What about Grandma, Pappy? What did she do?" I asked.

"Well, when Sheridan's men were roaming and plundering through the Valley, a Yankee soldier on his horse crossed the creek near our house. I remember seeing his horse slip on a flat slick rock in the creek. As he rode on up to our house, my ma was standing by the woodpile. He came up to her and asked, 'Where's your ole' man?'

"Ma replied, 'I don't have an ole' man; and anyhow, it's none of your business.'

"Again the Yankee asked, 'Lady, where's your husband?'

"I'm not gonna' tell you anything, and if you don't get away from here I'll chop you with this ax!' With those words she jerked the ax from the chopping block and brandished it at the soldier as he sat on his horse shouldering his gun. For some unknown reason the soldier left and didn't bother her any more. Ma was a very fearless woman."

As Pappy perused his memory, I turned to Mother and asked, "Do you remember the Civil War?"

Mother replied, "No, I was not born until after the Civil War in the year of 1869. I am ten years younger than your Pappy. Did you know that I went to school to him when he taught at Stony Lick?"

Frances spoke up, "No, I didn't know that. Was she a good pupil or a bad pupil, Pappy?" she asked.

Pappy laughed, "I guess I'd better not tell on her."

Turning to Mother, I remarked, "I bet you were his favorite pupil."

Again Pappy laughed, "She was then, and she still is, my favorite."

Soon thereafter Pappy guided Chester into the gate at our home.

Dreams and Fancies

The next morning Frances awoke with an upset stomach; she seemed to have a weakness for this ailment. Uncle Charlie our family doctor often referred to it as "summer complaint". Thoughts must have occurred that perhaps there had been too much Harrisonburg yesterday, however, no one expressed such. She didn't seem to want any breakfast and just lay around on the couch in the front room.

Mother decided she needed to give her something to settle her stomach and bowels. "I believe I'll fix her some nutmeg in boiling water and give her a few doses."

This remedy was made by grating one half of a nutmeg in a cup, then scalding it with a little boiling water, and after it had cooled, adding a bit of flour.

"Goodness! I don't have hardly any nutmeg! Esther, come here quickly! I want you to run down to Aunt Mag's and see if you can borrow a nutmeg. Now don't stay for I want to start giving some to Frances," instructed Mother.

My sunbrowned feet scuttled to the Crossroads and down the lane to Aunt Mag Showalter's house. Frances Diehl met me at the back porch door—back porch doors were the entrances on all farmhouses that were used by most errand runners. One of the necessary reasons for running errands was borrowing and lending. Shopping malls had not yet made their advent into community life; and sixty, seventy, hundred miles per hour modes of travel were still science fiction.

"Come on in, Esther," invited Frances.

I followed her into the kitchen where Aunt Mag was busy with her hands, kneading a bulky lump of bread dough.

Remembering Mother's instructions to hurry, I immediately said, "Mother wants to borrow a nutmeg. Frances has an upset stomach and she needs some."

Aunt Mag continued working her dough as she instructed Frances D. to get a nutmeg out of the safe for me.

Frances D. accompanied me out the door and into the yard as I made my departure. Frances D. was Aunt Mag's granddaughter and had come to live with her and her bachelor son Edwin when she was a small baby. She grew up with our family and was ever and always a close friend, along with the Bowman children whose home we reached by a footpath up a steep hill just beyond Aunt Mag's place. This closely knit trio of families provided much joy and happiness throughout all the days of our childhood and growing up.

As we approached the yard gate, Frances D. begged, "Esther, can't you come down and spend the night, tonight? Margaret and Elizabeth (the Bowman girls) are coming; we could have lots of fun."

Spending nights with friends was one of the simple pleasures and activities in which we loved to participate, so my response was one of anticipation and hopefulness, "I think I can, but I'll have to ask Mother; I'll call you as soon as I can." With that I scampered back up the lane and home.

Mother grated the nutmeg on a little tin grater, then placed the leftover piece in the little compartment at the top and pressed the lid shut to save what remained. She mixed her prescription of nutmeg, hot water and flour. Frances, who was usually ready to eat almost anything offered her, was rather reluctant to swallow this concoction, but with Mother in control, she had little choice. After periodic doses of it throughout the day she was feeling somewhat better by evening, whether because of this potion or in spite of it.

By that time I was on my way to spend the night with Frances D.—empty-handed, no tooth brush or tooth paste, no hair curlers, no pajamas; we slept in our brown cotton drawers or long underwear, depending on the season.

When Margaret, Elizabeth and I had arrived we began to shell home-grown popcorn, while Frances D. got out a heavy iron skillet and threw a couple sticks of wood in the cook stove to rekindle the fire. The corn popped like bullets against the lid of the skillet as she moved it rapidly back and forth across the flame in the open hole of the stove. Finally, we had a big bowl full, enough to satisfy our appetites for the evening. For a time we played "Silly Sentences," with Aunt Mag participating in the final composition: "Frances D. and Gramama/under the kitchen table/at midnight/picking potato bugs."

At last, at our insistence, Aunt Mag began spinning stories of her childhood for us. In time, when she began feeling tired and sleepy and ready to retire, she reminded us that it was bedtime for all. Margaret and Frances crawled in one and Elizabeth (who was ever my best childhood friend) and I in the other. After our usual whispering and giggling Margaret and Frances quieted down, but Elizabeth and I, being still young and frisky as new born "hootchies" (colts) and not ready to settle, continued to confide our innermost thoughts and secrets to each other.

"Elizabeth," I quizzed, "What do you wanna' be when you get big?"

Elizabeth pondered the question for a few seconds and then responded, "I guess I might like to be a nurse, I sure don't think I could ever be a schoolteacher like your sister Elizabeth. There's not many things a girl can do. What are you gonna' be, Esther?"

"Well, I use to think I was gonna' be a schoolteacher like Elizabeth, but now I've changed my mind. I'm gonna' be a movie star. I think I'd lots rather do that than be a schoolteacher. Yesterday when we were in town I saw some pictures of Mary Pickford outside the theatre. She is so beautiful, and she had on all those fine clothes. They call her 'America's Sweetheart.' She is playing in 'Rebecca of Sunnybrook Farm' now. Wouldn't it be fun to play 'Rebecca' and 'The Girl of the Limberlost' and all of those characters?"

"Esther, I betcha' your Mother and Pappy would never let you be in the movies."

"I don't know; I haven't told them. You are the first one I'm tellin' it to, so don't go around blabbin' it to anyone yet. You know something? They are lettin' me go to see the movie of 'Rebecca' tomorrow night with Jasper and the girls 'cause I have read the book. If I make all that money maybe I could help my parents so they wouldn't haf'ta work so hard. If I could have a big beautiful house like I read that most of them have, maybe they could even come to live with me. Anyhow that's what I wanna' be. Now promise me you won't tell what I just told you."

"I promise; I cross my heart I won't tell anybody," Elizabeth affirmed. But by now, tiring of that subject, her active mind was already beginning to conjure up other ideas. "Let's go over and tease Frances and Margaret. They act like they're asleep, but I bet they're not."

We slipped quietly out of bed and tiptoed over to them, but couldn't suppress our giggles as we clutched the foot of their bed and began to shake it.

"You'all go on back to bed," ordered Frances, "Uncle Edwin or Gramma might hear and get after us."

"Elizabeth, if you don't get in bed and hush up I'll tell Mother on you!" scolded Margaret.

"We'll go to bed," we said as we jumped on their bed with them. After the second dumping onto the floor we gave up and climbed back into our own. In no time we were sleeping the sleep of the young after a period of healthy fun and activity.

The clock on the mantle in the living room ticked away the minutes and hours in measured rhythm, but to one who lives in anticipation rather than for the moment the hands crawled along at the pace of an inchworm. I suffered from this affliction the day we planned to see the movie of "Rebecca." Mother finally said, "Esther, you must settle down; you are as fidgety as a boy with a burr in his pants."

Somehow I never could respond to her suggestion to settle down. When the time came to pile into our Maxwell, I suppose the burr was still in my pants. Jasper sat stiffly at the wheel, with Elizabeth in the front seat by his side. Bertha, Ruth, Mary and I occupied the back. I squeezed in on my ten inches at the edge of the seat and propped myself up by holding on to the back of the seat in front. I would not have complained if it had been necessary for me to sit on the floor at their feet.

After Jasper parked the car I stumbled over the others to be the first one out; and secure in my remembrance of the location of the theatre, I launched out in the correct direction. In my haste I began to outdistance them, zigzagging around the people on the street, until Elizabeth called, "Esther, wait a minute; don't be in such a hurry; we'll get there in time."

The facade of the theatre was just as I had remembered it on our trip a few days earlier—there was Mary Pickford, "America's Sweetheart" in all her beauty, on one side of the entrance, and on the other as the young, impetuous, lovable Rebecca.

We went into the semi-darkened theatre to the sound of the music inside. Happily, for me, the lights were soon turned off and the soundless black and white projection began—no ear splitting rock music, no bang, bang of guns and rockets, no zoom of airplanes, not even the sound of human voices—just the silent flashing of pictures on and off the screen with the script written at the bottom.

First, there were the short clips of the important items of current world news by "Pathe News Weekly":

Germany Agrees to Sign Peace Treaty Unconditionally
Prohibition is Effective June 30 at Midnight
Meuse-Argonne Fight Claimed 120,000 Men
Casualties During 47 Days Equalled 10% of Total Engaged
American Share 48,900
President Wilson Sails for U.S. Shores

This was followed by a comedy, "You Couldn't Blame Her," starring Harold Lloyd. Comedy and slapstick were very popular in the early years of motion pictures, it was usually clean, unadulterated fun.

We were then given a preview of coming attractions.

I heaved a sigh of relief when the screen flashed "Rebecca of Sunnybrook Farm" starring Mark Pickford, "The Darling of the Screen." From then on my eyes, my mind, my emotions, perhaps the whole of me, were transfixed by the pictures that appeared before my eyes. I had no difficulty reading the script at the bottom of each frame:

> The stage rumbled to the side door of the brick house and Mr. Cobb handed Rebecca out like a real lady passenger.
>
> "Rebecca Randall!" exclaimed Emma Jane, "you're handsome as a picture!"
>
> Rebecca sat down heavily in her chair as Aunt Miranda listed all her transgressions.
>
> I'm sure you must be Mr. Aladdin in the Arabian Nights," answered Rebecca.

And right down to the last picture when:

> Mr. Aladdin looked at Rebecca with adoring eyes and said, "I'm glad I met the child, proud I know the girl, longing to meet the woman."

That night as I fell asleep my dreams were a mosaic of life as Rebecca in Maine and Mary Pickford in Hollywood.

The next morning the unrelenting routine of farm life quickly propelled me back to reality. Jasper announced that he was going to cut the hay while the weather was dry.

"I'll need one of the girls to turn the grindstone for me. The mower knife will have to be sharpened before I can get at it," he announced, turning to Mother to supply his need.

"Oh, oh," I thought and Mother fulfilled my suspicions before I scarcely had formed them.

"Esther, you can do that as soon as you and Frances have cleaned up the breakfast dishes, if Jasper is ready then," Mother said looking in my direction.

How I dreaded the morning facing me! If there was one job I hated more than milking, it was turning the grindstone. Thank goodness it was needed only once or twice a year! It always took so long! But after the privilege given to me the preceding night, little opportunity was left for me to grumble, which we all did on occasions over the assignment of chores. Our complaints were unsuccessful most of the time, for Mother and Pappy were firm in their orders and had learned to ignore our fuming and fussing. "Hard work never killed anybody," Pappy frequently reminded us.

Sometimes I was unresourceful enough to remove myself from the scene of a chore, but now there was no escape path. Neither was there a genie to make me disappear in a cloud of smoke. Thus when Jasper called that he was ready I joined him at the grrndstone by the woodpile. In his hand he held the long mower knife with its blades set in a zigzag fashion. He slopped a little water onto the huge stone from the bucketful with which he had supplied himself. I began turning the handle as Jasper placed one edge of a knife against the stone, and the timeless process began. All the way down the cutter, the parallel sides of each blade were sharpened, but the time consumed was considerably lengthened as Jasper frequently tested the cutting edges with the thick part of his thumb and intermittently sloshed a bit of water on the stone. When he reached the end of the long knife and seemed satisfied with the edge of the final one, I thought, "Glory be! At last we are through!" How mistaken I was! He merely switched the ends of the knife around and started on the opposite edges of the blades.

I tried turning the handle faster but that didn't work—Jasper wouldn't allow it. I tried complaining that I was tired, that didn't work either—Jasper ignored it. He just let me suffer through to the end without any sympathy.

As the stone turned round and round, thoughts also began to tumble round and round in my head, thoughts not at all compatible with the rotating of the big wheel:

"I bet they don't have grindstones in Hollywood, and if I ever get there I'm not gonna' have one by my woodpile either."

"I'll have servants to do all the hard work for me."

If I could have put my thoughts into modern language I might have concluded that after all the practice I might be classed as a honing specialist or a grindstone technician.

I peered at my face in the somewhat diffused, bespecked mirror in our bedroom ("ours" was Bertha, Ruth, Mary, Frances and me.) As I surveyed the face reflected there, I thought, "My eyes aren't too bad; they are open and round and almost blue.'' I had often longed for eyes like Pappy's that were as blue as the sky on a clear day or Mother's hazel ones, so dark, deep and reflective.

'My nose turns up a little on the end, but maybe if I pulled it down occasionally I could give it the right angle.''

''My hair is awful straight, I wish it were pretty and curly like Frances'; and it is a nondescript shade of brown, but curlers and dye could probably take care of that.''

''My jaws are square and prominent; Mother says they have a determined look; my brothers and sisters say it is a stubborn look.'' I tried letting them hang loose; that seemed to help a little. ''Maybe I could practice that,'' I decided.

''My eyebrows sure do come together close over the bridge of my nose and fan out sort of like a cowlick. Mary Pickford's were arched in such a pretty thin line, I guess she does something to them to make them look like that.'' I knew nothing about the instrument that beauticians used to pluck them with so I leaned forward the mirror and caught one eyebrow between my thumb and forefinger and gave a healthy jerk. ''Ouch!'' I cried aloud.

''Esther, what are you doin'?'' asked Frances who had slipped into the room unbeknownst to me and caught me unawares, so absorbed was I in improving the image before me.

''None of your bizness; get on out of here and take care of yourself. Leave me alone!'' I fumed.

''I think I know what you were doin' and I'm gonna' tell Mother.''

''You'd better not, 'cause if you do I'll tell Mother about your buyin' candy with your Sunday School pennies.''

''All right, Esther, I won't tell her,'' Frances agreed. Then she suggested, ''Esther, let's dress up in old clothes.''

''Well I guess so. I'll tell ya' I'll be a movie star, that's what I'm gonna' be when I grow up. You can be the hero in my picture and I'll be the heroine.''

''Aw, Esther, I don't wanna' dress up in no man's clothes, they are too itchy and hot, and besides the suspenders keep slippin' off my shoulders and my britches fall down.''

''Well then I'll be a movie star and you can be my maid; I'll let you help me dress and you can brush my hair.''

''Oh, all right,'' Frances grudgingly consented.

When we stepped out onto the upstairs back porch we saw the older girls hanging up the last of the clothes on the yard fence.

Bertha spotted our activity and called up a warning to us, ''Don't you girls be gettin' into our pins and losin' half of them!

We don't have any to spare!" She didn't know that we had already helped ourselves, but she did know our past record.

"We're not gonna' lose any of them!" I called back. But pins did have a way of falling between the cracks in the floor boards and disappearing.

For a short while we clattered around in shoes too big for us, skirts too long for us, and waists whose bosoms we were unable to fill.

It wasn't long before Frances became piqued at the orders I was giving,

"Sophie, pin my skirt for me!"

"Sophie, bring me my button shoes!"

"Sophie, brush my hair awhile!"

Besides, she never enjoyed any project for a very long period of time, so we dumped our old clothes in their storage box and put the remaining pins that hadn't fallen between the cracks back in the pin tray on the girl's bureau.

Dog Days and Farm Chores

As the summers came and went in our valley they always brought with them the so-called Dog Days—and so it was in the summer of 1919. No youngster ever looked forward to this period with any anticipation. It occurred midst the hottest and most depressing part of the summer. All the parents still clung, at least in a measure, to an old superstition about Dog Days; the concept was that children were more susceptible to certain illnesses in this interval—summer complaint, breaking out with sores. They surmised that going in the creeks added to this susceptibility, thus they adhered somewhat to the custom of disallowing these excursions until we were no longer under the influence of the Dog Star.

To further our discomfort this was a busy time on any farm. There was field and garden work: pulling weeds, hoeing vegetables, picking off potato bugs, replanting the ground with sweet corn and beans, followed by fall crops, turnips and endive. This is the time of year when farm families plow out their year's supply of potatoes, when they make hay and haul wheat into the barns. Through Dog Days and beyond, household chores are just as numerous and demanding.

It's to be admitted that the Pence assortment of age and sex was ingenious enough to conceive of times and activities for some fun. There were neighbors, Frances D. and the Bowman children, plus other friends and cousins that we could make plans with, and we generally maximized these opportunities.

The summer that I fantasized about Mary Pickford and Hollywood, Dog Days came in with a vengeance. The sun came up each morning over the Blue Ridge in a cloudless sky. By noontime it seemed to stand still over head, beating down on the Pence farm and all our valley between the two great mountain ranges, the Allegheny and the Blue Ridge. Many days the temperature reached ninety degrees in the shade of the big black-bottomed apple butter kettle hanging on its wooden peg by the washhouse door.

Some days were so still there was no breeze to turn the windmill that pumped the water for the horses and cows at the barn.

In the meadow the cows huddled together under the trees, or stood ankle deep in the almost dry creeks. They seemed to be wooden animals, they were so motionless.

The chickens scratched bowl-shaped holes in the loose dirt around the woodpile and squatted in them to cool their hot bodies

Old Tom and Mother Cat crawled under the porch and stayed there; Jake said they weren't worth a hoot for catching mice in the barn anymore. That was usually their favorite sport.

Wilbur and Jake could no longer torment the old fat toad that usually sat in Mother's flower bed. He must have found a cooler spot somewhere.

The corn in the field rolled up into long green tubes as if it were hiding from the hot rays of the sun.

Even the birds seemed not to have the will to sing anymore as they sat on their perches among the limp motionless leaves.

And at night we children would stretch out on the cool grass in the yard. We didn't have enough energy left to chase the lightning bugs flitting around us.

But the bees swarmed over the ripe apples on the trees in Pappy's orchard. At least they never seemed to stop working, nor did the work on the farm ever seem to end.

Jasper and Pappy had finished mowing the hay and they and the younger boys had raked it in windrows to dry. Later, piling it high on the big wagon they hauled it in the barn. Hoping to catch a little breeze, Wilbur and Jake climbed to the top of the load and rode to the barn.

As Jasper drove the horses pulling the first load up the barn hill and onto the barn floor, Pappy called, "Girls, we are ready for your help now."

Mother in turn called to me, "Esther, you take the first time, so run along."

After finally finishing the dishwashing, I had installed myself on the back porch with "Mrs. Wiggs of the Cabbage Patch," my current novel, and was already engrossed in reading. I reluctantly placed a strip of newspaper as a marker in my book and closed it. Then I trudged slowly to the barn to do Pappy's bidding. Jake and Wilbur were in the haymow and Jasper was on top of the wagon load of hay. He plunged the huge fork suspended from the high point of the barn into the hay. Then Pappy led Chester, the horse, pulling the rope that lifted the fork with its load. When the rope became taut, the fork with its large clump of hay moved by means of pullys along the ridge pole of the barn until it was suspended above the mow, where its cargo was released and dropped. It was Wilbur's and Jake's job to disperse the hay evenly over the mow. Pappy led the horse back up the barn hill and my job was to pull the slack of rope up the hill behind the horse. This process was then repeated many times, and my work became a routine until the wagon was emptied of its contents.

At this point, the men returned to the field for another load and I to the back porch to continue my reading. I would have some respite while the men loaded the wagon again and Frances took her turn at pulling the rope. Once more I was soon immersed in Mrs. Wiggs' Cabbage Patch. There was no pastime that gave me more pleasure than reading—anything that was available. Our reading resources were so limited that we read some books over and over again.

The haymaking was completed. Sometimes there was a lull between the doing of major projects on the farm. This frequently allowed us at the time and freedom to draw upon our unrestrained wellspring of ideas. The afternoon ahead of us was just such an interim, thus we made our plans. Mary went to the telephone to call Frances D. who was on the same party line with us, therefore, we did not have to go through the switchboard to contact her. All that was necessary was to ring the correct number of longs and shorts and wait for her to signal her answer.

"Frances we want you and the Bowman girls to come up this afternoon so we can play games for awhile and then go to the orchard to eat apples," invited Mary. "We have finished making hay, so maybe Jake and Wilbur and Esther and Frances can play with us."

Frances quickly consulted her Gramma and answered in the affirmative.

When Mary had hung up the receiver she said, "Frances can come. We don't need to call Margaret and Elizabeth; Margaret was listenin' in on the line and said they could come too."

When our playmates arrived we got in a huddle to decide what we should play; "Sal in the Mush Pot" was the winner. We trotted out to raid the woodpile of its uncut limbs for potential sticks we could use for playing the game. Finally, everyone seemed to have a satisfactory implement.

Wilbur pulled a string ball from his pants pocket. "We can use this ole' ball, it's not much good anymore," he allowed.

We had a method for making string balls; as we unraveled one of the men's worn heavy cotton socks we simultaneously wrapped this yarn on something round and solid, hopefully a small hard rubber ball. After wrapping round and round the core to make a sizable ball, we secured the string by sewing over it many times with a darning needle and it was ready for many hard knocks.

Bertha dished out a big bowl-shaped hole and we formed a large circle around it with some distance between each player.

Frances D., ever the jolly good sport, volunteered, "I'll be 'it' this time."

"All right, Frances, let's see you hit the ball in the hole!" yelled Wilbur.

"Yeah, Frances, I wanna' see ya' put the ball right in that hole, right there!" challenged Jake, pointing with his stick.

Bertha cautioned, "Now everybody mind what you're doin' and keep the ball out of the circle."

After we had knocked the ball a distance several times, Frances mentally planned her strategy. She slowly dribbled the ball a safe distance from the circle, then shouted, "Hey, Wilbur, you and Ruth watch out, the ball is comin' at ya' hard this time!"

All eyes were riveted on Frances, the ball, and the space between Wilbur and Ruth. At that instant Frances quickly swatted the ball between Jake and Margaret, catching them off guard. The ball shot in the circle, Frances followed it immediately and putted it into the hole.

Frances laughed and laughed as Mary accused good humoredly, "That was a dirty trick, Frances!"

We all joined in the laughter, for everyone knew that no rule of the game had been broken.

Several more took turns at being "it" as the game continued.

"Don't let her get the ball in, watch it, watch it!"

"Ow! Quit hitting me on the ankle like that!"

"Hit it away, Elizabeth! That'a girl!"

"Ouch! You cracked me on the shin with your stick!"

"Watch out! Here it comes!"

"Don't swing that stick so high! You're liable to hit somebody in the head!"

Finally after shins, ankles, and the ragged string ball had about all the punishment they could take, we decided to call off the game that seems to be an ancient version of golf and hockey combined.

We girls went into the front yard and sat down under the maple trees to cool off in the shade. The boys disappeared—to where we knew not.

Elizabeth and I were not predisposed to sit still for a very long period, even in the shade on a warm day, so shortly we took off for the orchard.

"Esther, you pick out an apple that you would like to have on any limb, anywhere, and I'll climb up and get it. Then I'll choose one and you get it for me," challenged Elizabeth.

Elizabeth liked to climb and I didn't. Elizabeth was a daredevil and would climb anywhere. I wasn't and I wouldn't. I was a scaredy cat, but I didn't want her to know it, so I agreed to her proposition.

Any apple I chose anywhere in a tree, and I tried to make it difficult, she scrambled after with abandon. Any apple I tried to reach for her I did so with tenseness and fear and I clutched the limbs with every muscle in my body.

Finally, when the other girls came to the orchard I heaved a sigh of relief. I felt sure they had saved me from falling to the ground to be crushed and broken, or even a worse fate, death. I felt much more comfortable sitting under the trees with my sisters and friends and the apples on a pile in our midst.

Bertha broke the news of her fall plans to Frances D. and Margaret and Elizabeth, "I'm going to the Academy at Bridgewater this fall. If I want to be a really good teacher I'll have to get some more education. Since there's no high schools close here anywhere, that will be the best thing to do. And it is a religious academy run by our church, and that makes it better yet."

"Gee, Bertha, I wish you didn't hafta' go, we'll sure miss you, it won't be half so much fun around here," lamented Margaret.

And Frances D. added a sentimental thought by reciting one of the little poems so often said and written in those times:

When you leave us and go far away,
We hope we'll meet again another day.

"Hey, that reminds me. I'll run into the house and get my autograph book and you can each put a verse in it," Bertha said, feeling the sentimentality of the moment. An autograph book in those days and times was made up of little poems and sentiments from dear friends with accompanying signatures. It was not at all concerned with the names of celebrities or famous people.

While Bertha was gone we each made our decisions on what verses we would write. Here are our contributions:

When you get old andugly as folks oft times do,
Remember you have a friend old and ugly too.

Your sister, Mary H. Pence

When you get old and ugly as folks oft times do,
Come over to my house and eat apple sauce.

Elizabeth Bowman

'Tis sweet to love,
But oh how bitter,
To go with a girl
When her dress don't fit her.

Virginia Bowman

Tie a mule to a tree
Pull his tail and think of me.

Your sister, Frances E. Pence

The ocean is deep and wide across,
When I get married I'll be the boss.

Your friend, Frances Diehl

When your school day life is over,
The happiest to you have been given,
May you pass through the school of life,
And graduate in heaven.

Margaret Bowman

Not vernal showers to budding flowers
Not autumn to the farmer,
So dear can be as thou to me,
My fair, my lovely sister.

Your sister, Ruth M. Pence

When you are washing in a tub,
Think of me and give a rub.
If the water is too hot
Think of me and forget me not.

Your sister, Esther V. Pence

After each one made her tribute to the autograph book Bertha said, "Thank you; I'll take this to school with me to remember you all by."

At that moment a couple of hard apples landed among us, one of them finding Ruth's back as target.

"Where did they come from?" Ruth exclaimed, as everyone looked up in the tree above us.

"Well I don't reckon they fell out of this tree," answered Frances D. examining one of the hard apples.

At that moment a second fusilade of apples landed.

"Ouch, that hurt!" squawked Margaret.

"Hey, I saw something move up there behind those old pippin trees," our sharp-eyed Mary exclaimed. "I'll bet Wilbur and Jake are up there hidin' in the grass. Those limbs drag so low to the ground they make a good hidin' place."

"I have an idea," Bertha began to think aloud. "Let's get our hands full of apples and sneak up there and get it back on them."

"Let's do," I said, quickly jumping up, followed by Frances, Elizabeth, Margaret and Virginia.

"Take it easy now," directed Bertha. "Wait 'til they settle down again, and then we'll have to be careful in sneakin' up on them."

We all sat quietly with our hands full until they had sent their next volley of apples. "Now!" said Bertha. Then we slinked quietly in their direction. As we neared our target, Jake and Wilbur popped up to fire their next volley of apple bullets. The instant they saw us they dropped their apples, turned tails and scurried away as fast as their big bare feet could go, a barrage of apples following them. As brave as they pretended to be, they weren't about to face such an adversary as a group of girls seeking revenge. They had learned ere now that their sisters were a force to be reckoned with.

Frances and I knew that the men were ready to haul the wheat to the barn and pack it in the mow, preparing it for threshing sometime later, and that again we might be called on to help in the process. We also knew that mother and daughters now and for some days to come, would be caught up in apple schnitzing for various purposes: drying for winter use, selling to accumulate a little extra money, making our winter's supply of apple butter. Perhaps that explains why on this early August Dog Day we dawdled in washing the breakfast dishes.

"Guess how many teaspoons there are here," I challenged Frances as I dumped the dish of knives, forks and spoons into my pan of warm water and homemade soap suds.

"I guess there are thirteen," said Frances.

As I put them into the rinse water I counted: one, two, three, four, five and on to fifteen. "You forgot the ones in the sugar bowl and apple butter," I reminded her. "Let's play the game that Ruth and Bertha used to play. Ruth told me about it," was my next suggestion. "Ruth said they would try to guess how many big spoons of water a cup or something would hold. So you guess how many this glass will hold."

Frances pondered seriously for a moment and then gave her estimate, "I think it will hold twelve spoonfuls."

I started dipping my dishwater into the specified glass generally spilling as much on the outside as landed on the inside. So as to be expected, her estimation was not very exact.

Not being very proud of her success, Frances was anxious for me to try, "You guess how many big spoonfuls Pappy's coffee mug will hold, Esther."

I pondered deeply for a moment and then gave my decision, "I guess it will hold fifteen spoons."

Frances began dipping from the rinse water with about as much care as I had used in my spooning. My guessing and Frances' dipping didn't coincide either.

"Girls!" Mother's voice came from the front room. "Finish up those dishes right away! You have been messing around out there for almost an hour!"

Of course she was right, and in the meantime the water had gotten cold, the soap suds had disappeared, and the grease was clinging around the sides of the dishpan. "What a mess, I thought!" And I pledged to myself that if I ever became a movie star I wouldn't do such dull jobs, but I would have maids to take care of work like washing dishes.

By the time Frances and I, at Mother's urging, had pulled our shriveled hands out of the dish water, the men had brought in the first load of wheat and were ready to unload it in the mow on the opposite side of the barn from the hay. Pappy had given Wilbur permission to help a neighbor, Mr. Huffman, a few days, for which he would receive pay. This meant that one girl would have to take his place to help with the unloading in the barn. Jasper tossed the sheaves off the wagon with a pitchfork, Jake threw them to whichever sister was on assignment, who in turn tossed them to Pappy. Pappy then packed the sheaves in the mow row after row and layer upon layer. As load after load came to the barn the layers went higher and higher and the work became more difficult. In the final stages, Pappy was packing the sheaves under the eaves of the barn and we were working quite high up near the roof. The heat was merciless up there and the bundles of wheat were prickly and heavy. By the time one had taken several turns at this task one felt the need of some Raleigh's salve for the hands and Raleigh's liniment for sore and aching muscles.

Even before the last load of wheat had been stored in the barn awaiting threshing, we began to schnitz apples and continued intermittently for some time. This chore always had its beginning with Frances' and my going to the orchard to pick up bucketful after bucketful of ripe apples. Our workshop was the back porch, away from the steam and heat of the black iron cook stove with its assortment of pots and pans and skillets. Hopefully, an occasional breeze might stray our way and blow away some of the sultry heat of Dog Days.

Sometimes we filled buckets with the schnitz, sometimes washtubs, depending on the use to which they would be put. The job can become mundane and tiresome. We attempted to make it less so by singing, by taking turns in reading aloud, and of course there was the frequent flow of conversation between mother and daughters.

However, we were not obsessed with sex and spent little time discussing the mating habits of the birds and the bees. The effect of the Puritan ethic on our social and cultural life made sex discussion something of a taboo. Yet, from our parents we learned our morals and ethics: we were taught that sex before marriage or having a baby out of wedlock was a sin; we learned that it was wrong to tell a lie; we learned the value of hard work, that idle hands are the devil's workshop; and we somehow felt that hell's doors were always open for the transgressor.

"Esther, you are peeling your apples awful thick, that's wasteful," Mother chided me.

"We have so many goin' to waste in the orchard might as well let the hogs have some. At least they eat 'em," I said trying to justify my carelessness. "Anyhow my hands are gettin' awful tired. Can't I quit for a while?" I begged.

"No, but for a change you and Frances can take your buckets and bring in some more apples from the orchard. We are just about out."

That wasn't exactly my idea of quitting, but this half offering was better than none.

As we returned from the orchard, Wilbur and Jake were approaching the house from the direction of the barn, but their loud, hearty, raucous voices reached our ears before they appeared;

Old Dan Tucker was a fine ole' man;
Washed his feet in a fryin' pan,
Combed his head with a wagon wheel,
And died with a toothache in his heel.
He went to the river and couldn't get across,
Paid five dollars for an old blind horse.

The horse wouldn't go and he bought a hoe.
The hoe wouldn't dig and he bought a pig;
The pig wouldn't squeal and he bought a wheel.
The wheel wouldn't run and he bought a gun;
The gun wouldn't shoot and he bought a boot.
The boot wouldn't fit so he thought he'd quit.

Wilbur took the porch with one leap, his big bare feet landing with a thud. Ditto Jake. Sneaking his hand into the bucket of schnitz between Bertha and Ruth, he grabbed a handful.

"Stop that!" Bertha cried angrily, as she cracked at his fingers with the back of her knife. "Cut your own apples!"

Jake figured he might be more successful in my bucket.

"Mother, make Jake stop it!" I fussed. "We spend all this time peelin' apples then you and Wilbur come in and eat half of em!"

"Mother, maybe you oughta' give each of them a knife and put them to work," Ruth suggested.

"Yeh, I bet that would get rid of them in a hurry," added Mary.

"Boys! Stop tormenting the girls!" ordered Mother. "Go away now. I'll bet Pappy has things for you to do at the barn. If you're out of a job I can give you one."

"Uh-oh, Wilbur, let's get outa' here!" Jake quickly suggested.

Off they raced to the barn, big bare feet slapping the hard ground in rapid sequence. The chickens flew in every direction at the two missiles hurtling at them with such speed. The boys quickly disappeared inside the barn.

When we finally put away our paring knives, our accumulation of containers in varying shapes and sizes, and the leftover uncut apples, I suddenly beheld my hands with dismay. My fingers were coated with a dingy brown apple stain, which no scrubbing with homemade soap could remove. I had on occasions seen my sister Elizabeth, who loved to have lily white hands, rub them with green grapes to remove the stain.

"Well," I thought, "If I'm going to be an actress I'd better start right now taking care of my hands."

Out to the grapevine I went, pulled off some green grapes and started rubbing.

Mother and Bertha, who had been observing my actions, looked at each other with amusement, and in low voices away from my ever listening ears remarked, "Esther thinks she's going to be a movie star. Frances said that's what she told her."

"Yes I've noticed that ever since she went to see Mary Pickford in 'Rebecca of Sunnybrook Farm' she has been more concerned about her looks and sits around daydreaming or with her nose in a book."

Mother's and Pappy's innate wisdom and years of experience with my older brothers and sisters had taught them much about the thoughts and fantasies of children and youth, consequently Mother didn't take my moods and ambitions too seriously.

Summer Ends and School Begins

Dog Days ended with completeness and finality. It rained! For two days it gently and steadily rained. How blessed our valley felt! It washed all the dirt, the grime, and even our sombre spirits away. We had a washed world! Even the farm animals responded joyously to the refreshing showers. The pigs, which had been hardput to find a mud hole to bathe in, rolled over in the puddles, squeeling their delight. The cows and horses left the protection of the trees and stood in the open pastures, letting the rain flow over their stolid frames, washing the dust away. Little rivulets ran down the hills and across the fields, filling the thirsty creeks once again.

It confined us to the house for two days, but no one complained; it was somehow comfortable for each to settle down for awhile and do his or her own thing.

"Girls, here are a couple of spools I just emptied. Do you want them?" Mother asked from where she sat at her sewing machine.

"Yeh, we'd like to have 'em, maybe we can get Jasper to make us tops out of 'em," I answered.

"Hey, Jasper," we called. "Will you make us tops out of these spools Mother gave us?"

Jasper consented, "Might as well, can't do much out of doors this kinda' weather."

He got an extra piece of wood, along with his pocket knife, and began to whittle. Jasper was clever with his hands and was kindly disposed toward his two young sisters. He cut the flanges off one end of each spool, then whittled the remainder down to a point. He trimmed spindles to a size that fitted in the holes of both, pushing them through to the pointed end and trimming them to a point also. He left this spindle long enough to provide a handle at the upper side. When he finished he had two well balanced symmetrical little cones. Our unskilled fingers tried spinning them, with Jasper occasionally trying to show us how it should be done. I rather think that he, too, enjoyed seeing how expertly he could manipulate his handiwork.

By late evening of the second rainy day the downpour seemed to have slackened, and Mother stepped out onto the porch to assess weather conditions. On her return, she remarked, "I think it is going to clear up soon. There is a patch of blue in the sky big enough to make a pair of overalls. That's a good sign."

Mother was right, the next day dawned fair and bright. Just a day to go over to Uncle Joe Pence's to play with Marie—so Frances and I thought.

"Mother, can we go over to play with Marie this afternoon?" I asked. "We haven't been over there for a long time. Maybe we can go in swimmin' while we're there. Dog Days are gone now, and it sure would feel good to get in the water once again."

"Yes, I think it will be all right for you to go, but I'd rather for you to wait 'til the older children get there before you get in the water. They are planning on a dip in Uncle Joe's 'crick' later on this afternoon."

It was early afternoon when Frances and I started on our way: through the stubbles of the recently mowed hay field—along the rail fence where the daisies, blackeyed susans, and queen anne's lace mingled in peace and tranquility—over the face and across the hills and meadows of our pasture land—and from thence into the cool damp woods that separated our farm from Uncle Joe's. When we emerged from the shade of the locusts, pine and oaks, the tall three storied brick farm house came into view.

This house had always enchanted me. Grandpa Pence had built it many years ago and had moved his growing family, including our Pappy, from their log house across the creek into the new one. It snuggled against the hillside, providing the setting for two ground level entrances. A porch ran across the front of the second level, which was the company entrance. It was to this porch that Marie took us now, where we could visit and discuss play plans for the afternoon. We sat in the wooden porch swing, feet dangling at the end of legs not quite long enough to reach the floor.

"Let's go up to the chicken house awhile," was Marie's first suggestion. I never understood her fascination for the chicken house. With all its hazards and illwinds, I thought it a most unfascinating place.

"I'd rather go down and play in the crick," I hedged, "That's lotsa' fun."

"I would too," corroborated Frances.

"Let's go to the chicken house awhile first, then we can go to the crick," Marie suggested.

"All right, let's go then," I finally agreed, unwittingly learning how to compromise at an early age. My unexpressed thought was that it might just be better to let the creek follow the chicken house.

As Frances and I knew from first hand knowledge of a chicken house, there was no safe place to walk or sit, and the only potential for play was skinning the cat on bars used for roosts, and that was a bit risky. There are two kinds of chicken manure, so choose yours carefully—you have to smell it for a long time. Frances and I had learned that verity long ago.

We were quite agreeable when Marie, at last, did suggest that we go to the creek, which was a delightful place for creative play. There were flat smooth rocks, almost like table tops, that ascended one after the other in stair step fashion, and enough of them scattered along the creek so that we could each have our own little nook.

We visited and chatted back and forth:

"Come down to see me sometime."

"I have to go home and get dinner for my family."

"I need to clean house today."

"Haddo, come in and set a while."

"It's almost time for my children to be home from school."

Playing house continued until all the older ones had gathered to go in swimming (translating that word rather broadly). We all moved to the pool below the flood gate. We needed no bathhouse, for we more or less wore the clothes we had on. When Uncle Joe's four, Effie, Ethel, Virgil and Marie, plus seven of our family, Bertha, Ruth, Mary, Wilbur, Jake, Frances and I, jumped in the undersized swimming pool, the water level must have risen several inches. Even though space for maneuvering was limited, our pleasure was not. We considered this to be the best swimmin' hole in the community. It was deeper and the bottom was pebbly, thus preventing the water from muddying and clouding up.

Plop! I dropped into the water with knees clutched to my chest.

Plop! Went Marie.

Plop! Went Frances.

Splash! Went the water in all directions.

"Girls! Stop that!" ordered Virgil. "We are trying to swim!"

"You boys are pretty big splashers yourselves," accused Bertha. "You flap the water like an old hen that has fallen into the watering trough."

Marie, Frances and I contented ourselves by bouncing up and down in the water.

The older girls tried to find a spot of their own in which to swim.

Wilbur, Jake and Virgil, besides trying to swim, liked to challenge each other in performing their concepts of daredevil feats.

"I dare you to do this, Virgil," Wilbur challenged, as he stood on his hands with his feet sticking straight up out of the water.

"Watch!" Virgil shouted his reply, as he performed with equal skill.

"Now, Jake, it's your turn. We dare you to do it," they both taunted.

Jake paddled away without taking up the challenge.

After attempts at swimming, diving and splashing each other, Bertha took charge and reluctantly decided, "We'd better be gettin' home so we can get our work done before dark."

Late afternoon, and I was trying to finish reading "Sam's Chance" by Horatio Alger before time to gather the eggs and bring in the wood and chips to start the fire in the morning. I was propped up comfortably in the porch swing with a pillow behind my head, when suddenly I heard the front gate open. A man with an ax resting on his shoulder walked up to the porch where I sat. Not recognizing him as anyone I had ever seen before, and noticing his faded overalls and shirt and weathered leather shoes, I concluded that he must be a tramp. It was not unusual to see vagabonds roaming the countryside in this period of our nation's development. I can only guess that there were people who had a kind of wanderlust but no money or possessions or job, thus they adopted this life style. Their pattern was to travel the country over by hopping freight trains to some destination and then dropping off at a rural depot. The Grottoes and Port Republic stations were the jumping off points in our area. They seemed to have developed a perception of communities that would receive them with a measure of hospitality. It was often said that a Brethren would turn no one away from his door.

As the man approached the porch he spoke to me and asked, "Little girl, where's your pa?"

"I think he is at the woodpile cutting wood," I answered pointing in that direction.

The hobo walked with measured steps to where my Pappy was, and I dashed into the house to tell Mother about the stranger.

"Mother, a man just came to the porch and ask me where Pappy was. He was carrying an ax on his shoulder. I think he's a tramp," I informed her.

She glanced out the back door as Pappy approached the house.

"The fellow at the woodpile has asked for supper and breakfast and a place to sleep tonight," he said. "I agreed to let him stay if that is all right with you. I asked him if he would cut some wood in return for his bed and board and he agreed."

Mother nodded her assent and added, "One more place at the table won't make much difference. And I suppose we can put him upstairs to sleep in the boy's bedroom with them."

After this exchange of thoughts, Pappy returned to the woodpile where the man was already busy splitting wood. Mother turned again to preparations for supper, and I, along with my brothers and sisters, to completing the evening chores.

At supper that night this unknown, uninvited, but welcome stranger became a part of our lives for one short enchanting evening. He spun stories of places and adventures that we had never heard of nor knew existed. A travelogue of words that painted images for us.

"I have traveled from the Atlantic Ocean to the Pacific; I have seen the big factories and mills of New England and dipped my hands in the Gulf of Mexico; I have seen the snow capped peaks of the Rockies, and the deserts and the great plains of the West."

"Have you ever seen the Grand Canyon?" asked Pappy. "I often thought I would like to see it sometime. It must be a wonderful part of God's creation."

"Yes, sir, I have been there," he responded. "It is a great sight to see. It's impossible to describe what it's like to somebody else."

"Did you ever get caught in a blizzard or snow storm?" Bertha asked next.

"Yes, ma'am, one time in Colorado when an early blizzard came before I got on my way south. The wind blew so hard and the snow came down so fast I couldn't see two feet in front of me. If I hadn't stumbled into a logger's cabin I guess I wouldn't be alive today. I had to hole up there two days with nothing to eat, until the storm was over and I could be on my way again."

"Did you ever see a tornado?" was the next question.

"Yes indeed, I've had narrow experiences with them too, and I've gotten caught in dust storms out on the prairies."

When I had a chance to get a question in, I rather timidly asked, "Have you ever been to Hollywood?" Some amused glances turned my way at that question.

"Yes, little girl, I've been there a coupla' times. The place is full of movie people with great mansions. Such fine homes I never saw anywhere else. But some parts of that city are dens of iniquity," he warned.

"You heard that didn't ya', Esther?" Wilbur asked poking fun at me.

I decided after that answer it was better not to pursue this line of questioning any further.

As a precaution, Pappy took the man's ax and hid it in a corner behind the pantry door, though no one seemed to have any fears about this stranger spending the night in our house.

The next morning, before we had scarcely begun our chores, this wanderer disappeared down the road, out of sight and out of our lives.

Late summer seemed to be days in a hurry, they were moving so swiftly into yesterdays. We could see it everywhere on the farm. The tall grasses had become dry, brown and tired. Late apples had turned fat and rosy in Pappy's orchard, waiting to be picked. Mother's turnips and endive were growing in the garden, soon they would be the only green things there. One never knew when some early frost would sting the last vegetables of summer. Days were bright and warm, nights were turning cool. Fall asters and golden-rod were preparing to join the plants that had already bartered their blossoms for seeds or burrs or nuts.

One morning, on a walk through the chicken yard, Frances and I spotted some of these burrs, the large broad leaf dock plants that grew in big bunches there and formed their prickly tenacious little burrs with their pretty purple tams.

"Look, Frances!" I exclaimed. "Look at the burrs! Now we can pick some and make little baskets and other things. They are so pretty!"

"We sure can! Let's do it right now!" was Frances' immediate response.

We began pulling off the spiny burrs that irritated even our tough little fingers. As we gathered, we stuck them together to form little baskets, with the purple color to the outside. They clung together with considerable tenacity, each little barb interlocking with another. After forming the little bowl-shaped baskets, we stuck on a handle by which they could be carried. I was still working on my project when Frances stood up to admire her completed handiwork. But apparently she had not stuck the handle on securely, for at that moment the basket separated from it and dropped exactly on my head. The shot could not have been more accurate if she had taken careful aim and fired. There I squatted with a wad of burrs nesting in my thick, tousled, windblown hair.

"Now see what you did!" I yelled. "How am I gonna' get this outa' my hair?"

"I didn't mean to do it," apologized Frances. "It just came apart. I'll get it out for you."

"Ouch!" I squawked, "You're pullin' my hair! That hurts!"

The more Frances and I tried to get the mass of burrs out of my hair, the tighter it became enmeshed. The tentacles were those of an octopus refusing to let go.

"Now what am I gonna' do?" I asked becoming more and more exasperated.

"I guess we'll hafta' go in and ask Mother to get it out. Maybe she'll hafta' cut it loose."

"Don't say that!" I fumed. "I don't want a hunk cut out of my hair!"

But forgetting my burrs and basket for the moment, I stalked off toward the house with Frances following closely behind.

By the time I had reached the house tears were ready to overflow.

"Mother," I cried. "Frances let some burrs fall in my hair and we can't get them loose!"

"I didn't mean to," said Frances, who by now was almost as upset as I was. "I couldn't help it."

"I declare, what am I going to do with you girls? It seems that every time you play with burrs somebody gets them in her hair! Come here, Esther, let me take a look," said Mother.

"Ouch! That hurts! You are pullin' my hair!" I whined dancing up and down.

She was no more successful in dislodging the mess than we were, so she finally said, "Get me the shears, Frances, I'll just have to cut this out."

"I don't want you to cut my hair!" I wept. "I'll look awful with a hunk cut out! It'll be all crookedy!"

"I won't cut anymore than I have to. Now stand still, Esther!" she ordered.

"I bet it will take forever to grow out!" I wailed.

"I reckon it'll grow out before you get gray," teased Mary.

"Or maybe before you get married," Bertha added, bruising my pride still further.

Hurt feelings are usually healed, and pride sometimes takes a tumble. By afternoon I was almost back to normal; Frances and I were in the front yard still finding interesting things to do. Jenny Wren had vacated her house, swinging from the limb in the maple tree. There was a feeling of expectancy that fall was just beyond the next hill. As we followed the white paling fence around the yard, we discovered here and there a few audacious roses still defying weather warnings. The bush of little sweetheart roses had an abundance of tiny buds that would probably never unfold before Jack Frost came calling. Both of us began to pull them off to examine them more closely.

"I don't see any pink showin' anywhere, they sure are hard and tight," Frances observed.

"They don't have any color either, do you reckon they have any smell?" I asked, as I held them close to my nose.

Frances, trying to detect their fragrance, went a step further and stuck one in a nostril. "Hey, it just fits my nose hole," she observed and proceeded to stick one in the other nostril.

"Yeh, they do," I replied pushing one in each of my nostrils. "Maybe the smell will go straight up into our heads," I suggested.

"But I can't hardly breathe," said Frances and she began pushing at the buds to provide breathing space.

"It is kinda' hard to get your breath," I responded and I tried to adjust my rosebuds also.

No doubt most people have heard of the proverbial beans that children put up their noses—well the Pences never seemed to be quite traditional, so Frances and I chose rosebuds.

Shortly we began to realize that we were having trouble in getting them out. The more we poked at them the farther up our noses they went.

"Esther! I can't get these things out of my nose!" yelled Frances excitedly.

"What are we gonna' do?" I cried in fright, "I can't get mine out either!"

By now we were very frightened and when we saw the sight of blood we really began to wail.

"I'm scared!"

"I am too. What will Mother say?"

But in spite of what we thought might be the consequences of our actions, we dashed through the yard, across the porch and into the house.

"Mother! Mother!" we screamed. "We got rosebuds up our noses and we can't get them out!"

"Rosebuds! My goodness, girls!" Mother exclaimed. "What on earth were you doing? Come here and let me see."

By now she could see very little of the buds, but being an experienced mother she instructed us, "All right, girls, give a good hard blow."

We followed instructions and gave a good vigorous blow.

Slickened by the mucous that had formed in our noses because of our weeping, the buds finally popped out. Relieved, we wiped the tears and mucous away with our dress skirts, trying to compose ourselves.

"I don't know what you two girls are going to get into next," mused Mother. "It seems to me that burrs in your hair and rosebuds up your noses are enough pranks for one day. I think I'll have to put you in your beds to keep you out of mischief."

Bertha laughed, "I bet they would get their heads tangled up in their bed ropes if you did."

Mother, realizing that we were still upset over this latest escapade, softened her fun making, gave Bertha a look of caution, and said, "Girls, this hasn't been one of your good days has it? Wipe your eyes now and wash your hands, then go spread yourselves some butter bread and I'll put a little brown sugar on it." She knew that was one of our favorite treats.

"I guess it's about time to be getting supper, girls," continued Mother turning to the older ones. And she added, "I was just thinking before Esther and Frances came in that maybe we ought to have Uncle Joe's over for dinner Sunday. We haven't had them yet this year. I'll believe I'll call Aunt Fanny right now and find out if it suits them to come."

In a few minutes she joined the older girls in the kitchen and where Frances and I were waiting for our brown sugar.

"Well, I talked to Aunt Fanny," she informed us, "but it won't suit them to come." Then turning to Frances and me she gave the reason, "Marie has come down with the chicken pox."

Frances immediately had the explanation for this, "Well I don't wonder she has the chicken pox. Everytime we go over there to play she takes us in the chicken house."

At last we were all assembled and ready for the first day of school, new, old and patched blue denim book satchels, dinner buckets, and perhaps if Mother had taken time to examine, some questionable items in the boys' overall pockets.

We moved along at a brisk pace to the Crossroads, where we were joined by our neighbors, the Bowmans and Frances D., and set our course in the direction of Timber Ridge School, almost two miles away. The blue wood smoke curled out of farm house chimneys that silhouetted the landscape around us.

Conversation turned to speculation about our teachers, new or old, the grades we would be in, friends, and sometimes those we didn't want to claim as friends.

"I wonder what my new teacher will be like this year, I hear she is pretty tough. I hope she won't give me too much homework."

"I'm glad I'll have Miss Ruth again this year. I like her. She's nice."

"So do I."

"I'll be in Mr. Morris' room again, but he'll teach me some new subjects so's I can be ready to go to the academy at Bridgewater next year with Bertha," said Ruth.

"I bet fourth grade is gonna' be mighty hard," I worried.

"If you think fourth grade is hard, wait 'til you get to the sixth," warned Jake.

"I'm glad Mary and I are in the same grade again this year," said Frances D.

"Yeah, so am I, but it's too bad Wilbur will be around again," was Mary's comment.

Wilbur chided, "You oughta' be happy that I'll be around to keep you outa' trouble."

I turned to Elizabeth to express my thoughts, "I hope we can be deskmates again this year."

"So do I," responded Elizabeth, "I guess it will depend on how much talkin' and gigglin' we do whether Miss Ruth will let us set together."

"I guess I'll have to behave this year, Frances will be in the third grade and in our room, too. If I get into trouble, she will tell Mother and Pappy on me. She's a tattletale."

Frances, who had been listening in, countered, "You'd do it to me, too. You'd tell on me."

The banter continued until we entered our white institution of the three R's and school was officially opened in the fall of 1919.

We attacked the three R's with vigor and interest, plus the other subjects that were added as we progressed from one grade to another, grammar, hygiene, history and geography.

I was sitting at my desk furiously working on my fourth multiplication table. Frances' third grade class was having its reading lesson on the long recitation bench at the front of the room. Their story was one that Frances had heard and memorized when she was smaller from repeated readings by her older brothers and sisters. At that time she said it over and over to the delight and amusement of her siblings, for she had the habit of not pronouncing her r's, especially the initial ones, Thus, when it was her turn to read she zipped through the passage with great confidence, but reverting to her own original dialect:

> The boy he cied (cried)
> The huhy (hare) he cied
> Because they couldn't get
> the goats out of the eye (rye) field.

Tommy Crow sitting in the desk in front of me began to giggle, which infuriated me, the more so because he was not one of my favorite classmates. Consequently I whacked him on the back with my fist, at which point he yelped, "Ouch! Teacher, Esther hit me in the back with her fist!"

"Well you were making fun of my sister and that's not funny!"

"Tommy, you stand in the corner at the front of the room, and Esther, you stand in the corner at the back," Miss Ruth ordered.

That was neither the first nor the last time I ever stood in the corner for misbehavior, but I never ceased to be mortified.

Cold days turned into colder days, as autumn rushed toward winter. We bustled about doing our farm chores with alacrity. Bed covers came out of storage and were piled high over us as we slept in our unheated upstairs rooms. Long underwear became a necessary part of our wearing apparel, if not a welcome part. The flaps never seemed to stay buttoned and we could rarely fold the legs over smoothly in our heavy black stockings—our legs were lumpy from fall to spring.

I was sure that no one would ever wear long underwear in sunny warm California. Then it suddenly occurred to me that I hadn't thought about Mary Pickford and being a movie star for a long time. Hollywood now seemed far away in time and space.

Each twenty four hours seemed heaped with chores, challenges, routines and occasional surprises.

The day to day challenges were: to make a hundred on an arithmetic test; to be at the head of the spelling line and never to be turned down; to learn in my history book that the first permanent English settlement in America was at Jamestown, Virginia in 1607. I identified with the stories in my reader: "The Porcelain Stove" with the strange name, Hirshvogel; "The Little Post-boy," "Two Little Heroes," "The Christmas Cuckoo," "Tom the Waterbaby."

If I chanced to look in the diffused speckled mirror in our cold bedroom before dashing down the stair in my long underwear to dress by the warm stove, I observed my jaws as square as ever and my nose at its same turned up angle—and I knew it would always be so.

I felt secure with my family: my Mother and Pappy who watched over us, my brothers and sisters with whom I played and quarreled. My home was a haven, a refuge, and I was not ready to try my wings and fly away.

Rich man, poor man,
Beggar man, thief,
Doctor, lawyer,
Indian chief.

Housewife, teacher,
Missionary afar,
Nurse, "glad girl",

Movie
star.

Somewhere I lost a button.

PART TWO: THE YEAR OF DAVID LIVINGSTONE

Bible School and Commitment

Next to strawberry shortcake the Pences liked blackberry shortcake best. The blackberries that were our favorites were not blackberries at all but dewberries, at least in our vocabulary. They were fat and juicy and grew wild on brambles running along the ground in corn rows and hayfields that one must squat to pick—not at all like the better known variety that one can stand upright to gather.

And that was just what two of my sisters and I were doing on a summer morning yesterdays ago, squatting to fill our buckets from the bountiful crop ripening up and down the corn rows in the wheat field across from our farmhouse.

It sometimes seemed to me that I must have been born squatting and that I probably would die squatting. I squatted when I helped pick the tiny red strawberries for a shortcake a few weeks earlier. I squatted when Mother sent Frances and me to the orchard to pick up apples under the early harvest or strawberry red trees. I squatted when I helped gather the new peas or beans off the vines in the garden. I squatted on Saturday mornings when Frances and I had to give the kitchen and dining room floors their weekly scouring. And I squatted behind the wash house when I didn't want to go all the way down the path to the "little house" (outdoor toilet), and I didn't need the Sears Roebuck catalog anyway for my secondary performance.

In fact it occurred to me that we could even walk squatting, as we shuffled our bare brown feet along on the cloddy ground, without bothering to unfold our legs and stand upright.

The sun was now awhile above the Blue Ridge Mountains, and it was warm on my sunbonnet and faded gingham dress, whose color had long since disappeared in the wash tub from its many weekly scrubbings on a washboard with homemade soap, plus hangings on the line in the sun to dry. It was now my everyday dress, and it indicated that I had grown several inches since Mother had hemmed it for a school dress the previous summer.

Mary, whose back was turned to me, was busy pulling the clusters of berries off the briars several feet beyond. Frances, several feet in the opposite direction was not even squatting but sitting flat on her bottom in the dirt, busily eating the few berries she had collected in her bucket. I was tired, and since no one seemed to be noticing me, I finally unsquatted and stood up, unraveling my muscles in the process.

We were surrounded in all directions by shocks of wheat, a congregation of short, fat, lumpy people, petrified and motionless. The Blue Ridge to the east of us had grown hazy and more obscure, as the sun moved imperceptibly to reach the top of the sky above us. I pulled off my sunbonnet and the slight breeze ruffled my hair, while it ballooned my dress out from my petticoatless body.

"Esther!" Mary sharply interrupted my reverie in the middle of a sentence. "Stop your piddlin' and get to work! Do you reckon I'm gonna' pick all these berries by myself?"

"How about Frances?" I snorted "I think she ate all she had in her bucket and that hasn't filled her big fat stummick'."

"Aw you know Frances always does that! You never can get much outa' her. That's no reason for you not to help, so get to work!" ordered Mary, and then added, "I wanna' get these buckets filled. Mother said if we did that she'd make some preserves from the extra ones. I sure would like to have some in my school dinner bucket instead of apple butter all the time."

"I would too," I added, "But I bet Mother will put the preserves in the Sunday safe and save it mostly for company. That's what we always do."

Finally, Mary said, "Well, anyhow get to work and let's finish up. I think it's gettin' towards dinner time, and I'm gettin' hungry."

Frances had a ready addition to that, "I'm gettin' hungry, too. So listen to Mary, Esther, and get to work and pick some berries so's we can go home soon."

"Gee whiz, Frances! How could you be hungry? You've ate every berry you picked. If you eat anymore you'll turn into one!" Mary scolded.

"She's already doin' that from the looks of the color of her face and hands. She's already turnin' purple," I said disgustedly.

Frances circled her lips with her tongue and licked her sticky fingers as if to get rid of the telltale color, or perhaps to suck in the last vestige of the taste of dewberries.

After this little verbal exchange, we settled down filling all our containers as fast as our nimble fingers could work.

By this time we had traversed the width of the field and had to wend our way back to the house the same distance we had come, but this time carrying a heavy load.

"Now, Frances, don't you stumble and spill all those berries,"

Mary cautioned. "If you do I'm gonna' spank you!" she threatened.

And for once Frances carefully watched her steps and made it to the house with her unspilled bucket.

As we entered the kitchen Mother took notice of our full buckets and remarked, "My, girls, that's a nice lot of berries. They must have been plentiful for you to be able to find so many. We'll have enough for shortcake, and some left over for preserves. Now go wash up for dinner, I know you are hungry after all that work."

"Yeah, and hot and tired too," added Mary as she pulled off her sunbonnet and mopped her face on her dress sleeve.

"Me too! Me too!" said Frances. " 'Specially I'm hungry."

"How could you be hungry?" I shot at her. "Your stummick is nothing but a big puddle of berries now!"

"Now, Esther, don't be so hard on your little sister, remember she is not quite as old as you are. I expect there was a time when you didn't do so well either," admonished Mother.

By now Elizabeth called, "Dinner is ready! Come on to the table everybody!"

Our fingers were sticky and purple with juice. The briars we had worked among all morning had pricked our hands and arms and some of the tiny thorns still remained in the flesh, adding to the stinging sensation. We quickly scrubbed them with water and strong homemade soap, and made an attempt to dry them on the roller towel that was minus any dry spot after heavy usage by the rest of the family. The briars had just as mercilessly scratched our feet and ankles, but there was no thought of washing them until the required time, which was just before going to bed.

We all sat around our long dinner table, and after a morning of vigorous toil we ate with healthy young appetites the food set before us. There was no pampering of anyone's likes and dislikes or dumping of full plates into the slop bucket afterwards (we didn't know of garbage cans in those days).

One of the rewards for fulfilling a difficult morning assignment was the opportunity to sometimes have free time in the afternoons. Of course there were exceptions to this, when special tasks consumed a full day or days. Somehow we were usually creative and inventive enough to fill those minutes and hours with happy and interesting things to do and without gadgets, games, television, radios, stereos, ad infinitum.

When this day's opportunity came, Frances and I decided we would go and spend the afternoon at Margaret's and Elizabeth's house, with Mother's permission. This was forthcoming with an admonition to be home by four o'clock—and the inevitable one, be sure your faces and hands are clean before you go. Wasted words—the latter admonition, for by the time we had reached the Crossroads we had somehow managed to reverse cleanliness in favor of dirt.

From the Crossroads we skipped down the dusty lane to Aunt Mag's familiar house, along the wagon road to the creek, and from thence up the precipitous footpath to the Bowmans' house.

Margaret and Elizabeth met us at the door with, "Come on in."

We immediately told Cousin Edna, "Mother said to tell you that we should come home at four o'clock."

"Come on, let's go to the barn," Margaret suggested immediately. "We have a little 'hootchie' (colt) that was born last night. He is the cutest little thing. He can't half stand up. He wobbles around and looks like he is all legs."

"Is it a boy or a girl hootchie?" I queried, curious as always.

"It's a girl hootchie, least that's what Father said," replied Elizabeth.

"How does he know?" was my next question.

"He says he got it straight from the horse's mouth," Elizabeth replied, with childish confidence that her father knew most everything.

After watching the amusing antics of the awkward little animal, Frances suggested, "Let's play 'Hidey Who' " (the old version of Hide and Seek).

After rounding up the younger Bowmans, Carl, Virginia and Ruth, Margaret counted to see who would be it:

> Eerie, Irie, Acre, Ann,
> Filis, Folis, Nickris, John,
> Kribley, Krobley, Vergie, Mary,
> Singum, Sangum, Borney, Buck.

Bowman's barn was not nearly so frightening as the Pence barn. It was a rather low, one story type, not at all like ours with its high beams, tall ladders and back doors far above the ground. I felt safe and secure as we played on until, to our regret, Cousin Edna called, "Girls, it's time for you to go home now; it's four o'clock."

Supper was over and the dewberry shortcake platter had been literally licked clean. The evening farm chores were being completed as the sun sank behind the Alleghany Mountains to the west of us. The day just ending had been a hot one, hot enough to send the family to the front porch and yard in search of some cool breezes as night fell.

Wilbur and Jake tusseled and tumbled in the grass, but Mother and Pappy and the other grown-ups relaxed on the front porch. For a time, Frances and I indulged our bodies in the cool grass, sensing the blackness that hovered around us.

Perhaps only those who have lived away from the brilliance of city lights can know the vastness and solemnity of the universe at night. At this moment the only illumination in the darkness was the millions of stars above us and the pale shadowy lamps in the windows of the Bowman and Baker houses on the hills in the distance.

Frances and I were not inclined to be observant or contemplative for long. We began to chase the lightning bugs about the yard, catching them with our hands and dropping them in glass jars. As I watched their little lights flickering on and off I wondered what could be the use of them. Since they were tail lights how could they light the way through the darkness? Maybe they should fly backwards. And furthermore, if they wanted to see where they were going they should not be flashing them on and off all the time. Scientists tell us now that this process has quite a different function. Another question I had about lightning bugs was why in the world did they have to stink so much. At that point my hands smelled awful. I decided all that odor should not go to waste, so I walked over to Wilbur and rubbed them under his nose. "Don't they smell good?" I asked.

"Cut that out!" yelled Wilbur, cracking at my fingers. "You do that again and I'll rub a bug under your nose!"

I didn't wait for him to carry out his threat but took off to the house and washed my hands with strong soap. When I returned the others were singing, and since my energy had been expended by now, I sat down on the porch steps and joined them in carolling some of our favorite hymns and ballads, as we often did of a summer night.

At length Mother said, "Children, I think it's bedtime and since some of you are going to Bible School in the morning you'd better turn in. You'll need to get up in time to get your work done before you go."

"Daughters, you ought to dump the lightning bugs out of your jars before you leave," Pappy suggested. "We shouldn't kill harmless insects, and they will die if you leave them bottled up in those jars." His concern was there, even though thousands of them were glowing in the darkness around us as far as the eye could see.

Today I wonder, "Where have all the fireflies gone?" Of a summer night, as I look across the expanse of meadow fronting my house, I catch only an occasional blinking of lights from these little insects of the night.

The next morning Mother's usual call ascended the back stairs. "Children, it's time to get up! Come on down and get your milking and other work done."

I bounded out of bed immediately and pulled on my everyday dress, taking time to fasten only the top button; I was in a hurry, and besides, the others were too hard to reach.

As I dashed down stairs I could hear Wilbur and Jake in their room kicking and shoving, trying to jostle each other from their bed. This seemed to be a routine with them, and it's surprising that the bed withstood this wrestling match year after year. Mother often threatened them with making a pallet on the floor if their bed ever succumbed and fell apart. Their rowdy conduct did not distract me this morning, for I wanted to get my work done and be ready for Bible School on time. Opportunities for participation in such an activity were rather infrequent but always welcome.

Shortly after eight I was ready and waiting for my friend Mabel Mundy to drive by in her buggy and pick me up as we had previously planned. Jasper was to drive Mary, Wilbur, Jake and Frances in the car. Impatiently waiting for Mabel to arrive, I was up and down and back and forth to the window, until Mother finally said, "Quit fidgeting around, Esther, and settle down. She'll be along on time."

At last when she did arrive, I climbed in with my friend, and with a crack of the reins in her hands we were off. The way to our church was very familiar to me and good for thirty minutes of happy thoughts between friends, spoken and unspoken. Little puffs of dust arose with each hoof fall as the horse ambled down the hill. We forded the small stream at the bottom and soon approached the woods where we always gathered crowfoot violets in the spring. The road along the edge slanted somewhat precipitously toward the ditch, and I ofttimes had a sensation that the vehicle in which I was riding would slide off, especially if snow and ice were covering the ground. As we were wont to say, "It sure did lean towards Kagey's." I have no explanation or origin to offer for that expression. I knew the occupants of all the farm houses we passed, Miss Mellie and Miss Lula Pirkey, the Winegords, the

Bowmans, the Wamplers and Uncle Charlie Harshbarger's house and doctor's office. Here we made a sharp turn to the left, and from thence it was a short distance to the church.

Bible School was to be a real inspiration to me. Our teacher was Miss Mareta Miller, whom I soon learned to adore. Our main area of study was the life of the great missionary to Africa, David Livingstone.

From the beginning to the end of the study I became emotionally and romantically involved in the life and work of this great man called The Pathfinder: when he said goodby to his family at Glasglow, Scotland, in the year 1840 to sail thousands of miles of ocean to the then so-called Dark Continent of Africa; as he treked hundreds of miles over African soil through desert and jungle and mountain; his years under the blazing sun healing black children who were ill, teaching their fathers to read, to worship God, and to dig canals that would carry water to their parched gardens; the time he was injured by an attacking lion and the many times he faced hostile native tribes.

As each day brought new insights into his life I became more inspired by the work that he did, the sacrifices that he made, and the wonderful Christian that he was.

Once he had heard another missionary to Africa, Robert Moffat, say, "There is a vast plain to the north where I have seen in the morning sun the smoke of a thousand villages where no missionary has ever been." So "The Pathfinder" set out on his search to open a path through Africa. He was the first white man to see "Sounding Smoke," which he renamed Victoria Falls. Nothing could stop "The Pathfinder" of Africa until he had ended his quest.

Along with this study we also had Bible assignments to carry out. One day Miss Mareta instructed us to find a chapter we thought David Livingstone should read on one of his journeys. After dinner I took my Pappy's Bible off the shelf and with it in my hand I approached Mother. "Miss Mareta gave us some work to do for tomorrow. She wants us to find a chapter in the Bible that would be good for David Livingstone to read on one of his journeys. I'm going to do that right now."

"All right, go ahead and do it now, for later on you'll need to help Ruth pick a mess of beans for dinner tomorrow," replied Mother.

As I left Mother I collected my current book, "Freckles," from the couch in the front room where I had left it, tucked it under my arm and slipped into the parlor, hopefully out of sight and sound of the family. Our parlor was cool, dark and musty smelling, for the window shades were kept drawn except on Sundays. Then it was open for company, usually relatives, and for the beaus who called on my older sisters on Sunday evenings. The chairs in this room were too stiff and straight for comfort, so with my two volumes I stretched out on my belly on the red and green flowered carpet that covered the floor. I first tackled the assignment of finding the appropriate Bible chapter. This was not an easy task, since my familiarity with the Bible was not spectacular. I spent some time searching for one I thought would be suitable. After I satisfied myself with a selection, I marked the place and laid the Bible aside, then opened "Freckles," relaxed contentedly, and began reading.

Sometime later I heard Ruth in the distance ask, "Where's Esther? I'm ready to go get the beans now."

Mother explained, "She told me she had to look up an assignment in the Bible for Bible School tomorrow, but she ought to be through with that by now."

Mary interjected, "I bet she's somewhere reading a book and I bet it's not the Bible."

Afraid that Mary's statement might be proven true, I jumped up from my spot on the floor and hid "Freckles" under the photograph album on the table. Then I assumed the same position as before and opened my Bible again. However, this ruse failed to work for long, my hiding places were too well-known and too often used to be secret. Shortly I was squatting between bean rows with Ruth, gathering handfuls of long tender green beans.

At another session Miss Mareta called for volunteers to offer prayer the next day during opening exercises. Getting no response from the class she turned to me and asked, "Esther, will you do it?"

I was mortified that no one had responded to her first request, so in spite of my inward fears, I said, "Yes."

The anxiety and apprehension remained with me all the way home and through the afternoon, as I agonized over what I should pray about. I had never prayed in public before, such chores were usually performed by our ministers and elders, at least by adults (mostly male).

Sometimes we knelt by our beds and said our nightly prayers, but I must confess that this was not done with any regularity. The activity around us did not lend itself to much privacy, and the coldness of our rooms in winter did not encourage us to tarry long on our knees. I'm sure that God in his infinite gentleness and compassion understood the frailities of the young, sympathizing with our handicaps and excusing our missing prayer time.

I regretted when the day came for Bible School to end. When the time did arrive I had made what I felt was a major decision that would affect the rest of my life. I was touched by the selfgiving life style of David Livingstone and so captivated by the excitement of his adventures that I decided my future would be dedicated to this work. Yes, I would be a missionary.

As we sat around the dinner table on the closing day of school, Mother asked' "Did you children enjoy Bible School and did you learn something?"

"I liked it because we studied about Wilbur Stover who was a missionary to India. He has my name. It was kinda' interesting," Wilbur answered first.

"Yes, we named you after him; we hope you can honor his name and be a good and great man, too," said Pappy.

"I guess Bible School was all right," Jake reluctantly agreed. "But it was an awful lot like just plain old school."

"Yeah," agreed Frances. It was sure hot and I got tired just sittin'."

"But we had recess," I broke in. "And that way I got to play with some new friends, like Eva Long, Bessie Mundy, and Pauline Hinkle. Miss Mareta was such a good teacher, too. I didn't want Bible School to close; studyin' about David Livingstone was so interesting."

Since I didn't want to make the announcement of my decision before the whole family, being a little sceptical of their reaction, I waited until I could talk to Mother in private.

The opportunity was afforded me when Mother stepped out on the kitchen porch to mop her brow and catch a breath of fresh air. There were not many times in a day that Mother could be found in privacy and seclusion, since she was usually surrounded by her active family. I grasped the moment and followed her to the porch.

I had something to ask and something to confide. "Mother, could I use your Bible for awhile? I think I want to be a missionary when I grow up and I think I'd better be gettin' ready for it. I thought I ought to start reading through the Bible right now."

Little did I realize the course I was laying out for myself in the days ahead.

"Of course you can use my Bible. I'm glad you're interested in reading it. Why did you decide to be a missionary?"

"I just like the way David Livingstone lived. He was such a good Christian. And Cousin Ike and Cousin Effie are, too. They always look so happy and peaceful like they know they will go to heaven some day. I want to be like them." Cousin Ike and Cousin

Effie Long were missionaries to India and were members of our church and supported by it.

"I think it's fine if you want to be a missionary, but I hope it isn't just because you think it will get you to heaven some day. I hope it's also because you want to help people."

"Yes I do. David Livingstone was always helping people. He doctored them and taught them and helped them to get water on their land so's they could raise food. I learned about it in Bible School. Maybe I oughta' study to be a nurse and then I could really help others."

"That is fine if you think this is what you want to do. But of course you have a long time ahead of you to think about it. In the meantime you can learn to do your work well and be a good and helpful girl. Pretty soon it will be time for you to gather the eggs and for you and Frances to bring in your wood and pick up the corn cobs and chips to start fire in the morning."

I felt good after my self revelation to Mother and with my decision for the future. So without too much show of reluctance to perform my regular tasks or feelings of self denial of other more pleasurable activities I could be doing, I picked up the egg basket and went to the henhouse. On this afternoon I was even a little less antagonistic to our feisty old rooster and the fussy settin' hens. Likewise I refrained from accusing Frances of not picking up her share of the chips and corn cobs when we performed this chore.

We make no attempt however to record the number of times I fell from grace in the days ahead.

My opportunity to practice nursing and learn how to help people came sooner than was anticipated. A few days hence, Elizabeth complained of a headache and sore throat, and as was her wont to do, she decided to stay in bed until she felt better. Besides, she loved to be pampered and waited on, thus providing a perfect opportunity for me to be nurse. I immediately seized upon this opportunity. Mother approved, my older sisters indulged me, and Elizabeth, with her love for being waited on, played the game with me. Unknown to me, I was probably the most serious one in the whole act.

At the time, I had a baby blue checked gingham dress almost identical with the material in the dresses worn by the student nurses at the Rockingham Memorial Hospital. It was the most suitable outfit I had for my role playing. Ruth cut a cape collar out of a piece of white material in the shape of the ones the nurses wore and fastened it around my neck. Finally, she fashioned a cap out of paper and secured it on my head with hairpins. I was so pleased with my appearance, and I was now ready to take over the duties of nursing Elizabeth.

When mealtime came I got a tray and carefully arranged her dishes on it. Mother permitted me to get a cloth napkin from the drawer to place beside the dishes, and then I went to the front yard and picked the prettiest rose I could find and placed it on the tray to give it a touch of beauty and fragrance. Holding it carefully, I carried it upstairs to Elizabeth's room. Elizabeth humored me by allowing me to be every inch a nurse. I propped her pillows behind her back and placed the tray in front of her. While she was eating I busied myself about her room straightening up this and that, adjusting the window blinds and hanging up her clothes on the hooks by the door. When she had finished her dinner I again carefully set her tray aside and asked solicitously, "Can I do anything more for you?"

"Yes, nurse," she replied. "You can put another pillow behind my back and straighten my covers a little. Then hand me my book off the table there. I think I'll read a little while."

After I had complied as best I could, she expressed her gratitude, "Thank you, nurse."

We were mutually indulging each other and mutually enjoying it.

This seemed to be a ready-made beautiful situation, but I soon learned that beauty didn't extend below the bed where the little gray porcelain potty sat. Of course, I had always emptied my share of these vessels but hadn't reckoned with this being a part of my present glamorous job. However, when the occasion required the job be done, I dutifully carried it out. If it were one of those times demanding it I burned a string in the room to rid it of odors as I had seen my Mother do. There were no lilac or pine scented air fresheners in those days. Perhaps our burning string was just as effective. Could be that Elizabeth might have gone down stairs for this performance, but perhaps she wanted to contribute to my experience in all nursing chores.

On the afternoon of the second day, when Elizabeth seemed to be improving, hopefully from my care, I carried her empty dinner tray through the door to our bedroom where I heard Bertha moving about.

I asked, "What are you doin'?"

"I'm gettin' ready to go to a party," was her reply. "Ethel and Effie are coming by in the buggy to pick me up. I wanna' be ready when they get here."

As she stood smoothing back her hair, straightening out the bertha (a deep lace collar) on her yellow dress, and generally admiring herself in the mirror, I remarked, "That sure is a pretty dress you have on."

"Yes, I kinda' like it myself, and I think I look real nice this afternoon, maybe about the best I ever looked."

"You do look real pretty," I said contributing to her present vanity. Then I left her to admire herself in private.

At that moment Mother called, "Bertha, are you ready? Effie and Ethel are coming up the road. You'd better come on."

"Yes, I'm ready!" Bertha called back, giving her hair one last pat and dashing her nose with a powder puff.

Then she sprinted down stairs, dashed through the dining room and into the kitchen, her words tumbling out as fast as her feet moved, "Hey, everyone, how do you think . . . . ?" Bang! Into the iron pot of slop by the stove she stumbled. In one great crash she and the slop bucket clattered across the floor! And there she was, lying in a puddle of swill, swill in her hair and on her face, swill soaked the pretty yellow dress and her shoes and stockings and ran in thick smelling streams across the kitchen floor. In all her misery and humilation her feelings of guilt came out, "Pride goeth before destruction and a haughty spirit before a fall," she confessed. Needless to add there was no party for Bertha that day, but there was a major cleaning job and the pigs were minus one kettle of slop for supper.

A Visit and a Family Portrait

Frances and I had scoured the kitchen and dining room floors and had slipped out to the front yard while waiting for them to dry.

"Let's play 'Andy Over,' " I suggested. I had brought our string ball along hoping for Frances' cooperation.

"I'll play if you don't hit too hard with the ball," Frances agreed.

"I won't throw it hard; cross my heart," I promised. With this assurance, Frances stationed herself on one side of the quite high boxwoods that lined both sides of our front walk, and I on the other.

Since I had the ball in my possession, I started the game. "Andy over!" I shouted, and tossed the ball over the boxwoods.

"Over," she echoed back when the ball crossed the barrier.

If Frances caught the ball she would dart around the hedge and try to hit me with it. If she failed to catch it she would call "Andy over" and toss it back to me. Anytime either could catch the ball she would slip stealthily around the boxwoods and attempt to hit her opponent. If she were successful the game was won.

Since we weren't very efficient at this, any interruption that caught our attention was accepted.

"Hey, there comes the mailman, there comes Mr. Burgess!" I called, stuffing the ball back into my pocket as I ran to the yard gate. Frances followed.

The mailman was as familiar a figure in the neighborhood as the school teachers who confronted us so many days in the school year. And he was almost as constant in his appearance as the sunrise over the mountains to the east of us.

He drove up now in his buggy pulled by his faithful grayish white horse. Today his buggy top was folded back, for the day was sunny and warm. In the winter when the days were cold the top was up, and in inclement weather he often used a protective storm curtain. As he pulled up to our mail box, he smiled, which accented the lines in his tanned weathered face.

Handing us our mail he said, "Good morning, girls. I suppose you want your today's mail. You have a letter from your sister,

Grace, guess your mother will be glad about that. Here is your 'Daily News Record' and your Pappy's 'Capper's Weekly'; he'll be glad for them. The Capper's Weekly was a newspaper out of the state of Kansas which featured the farming, economics and politics of the mid-west. Pappy was always interested in country and world affairs and informed himself as best he could. The female side of the household also enjoyed this paper, for it contained items of interest to women young and old, as well as a weekly continued story.

Before Mr. Burgess drove off he added further, "Girls, tell your folks that your neighbor Bessie Smith is sick. I hope it's not typhoid fever again."

He was not only a mail carrier but a news carrier also. Not gossip, this was one of the means by which important news was sometimes transmitted through a community, news that might mean life or death to a neighbor.

Mr. Burgess didn't know how delighted we would be with Grace's letter, for it contained news that she would be coming home for a visit soon. Grace now lived in Montana, a place much farther away in those days of slow communications, and she hadn't been home for almost four years.

Mother's eyes filled with happy tears when she read the goods news. "Girls! Girls!" she called. Leaving our unfinished morning chores we all hurried to the kitchen where Mother was sitting with Grace's letter in her lap. "Listen to this," she said as she picked up the letter and began to read. "We are planning a trip home to Virginia. We will be driven from Froid, Montana to Williston, North Dakota and leave there by train for the East on Saturday, July 15, arriving in Staunton on Monday, July 17. We are anxious to see everyone. It seems like such a long time. Esther and Frances must really be growing up by now."

As Mother laid the letter aside, she continued, "Well, girls, it looks like we'll have a good bit to do between now and next Monday."

"We'll have to do some baking I suppose. Do we need to make another batch of bread?" Elizabeth asked.

"I'm sure we will," replied Mother. "It takes lots of loaves when that many are here."

"How about butter?" asked Bertha. "Do we have enough cream for a churnin'? There wasn't much left in the crock when I dipped out the last plate full."

"I think we can get together enough cream by the end of the week," was Mother's response.

"One more job for Frances and me," I thought, but didn't express this aloud for I too was excited and happy.

Mother continued her planning, "I'm glad the garden is coming in well at this time. We oughta' have plenty of beans and corn and tomatoes while Grace is here. And my cucumber patch is doin' real well now."

"Yeh, having three more in the family means fixin' a lot of extra food," Ruth said, adding her bit to the chatter. Jesse, their young son, would be coming with them. He was our first grandchild and nephew.

"Let's get up early on Monday morning and get the washin' done and out of the way before they get here," suggested Mary.

"That's a good idea," we all agreed.

"I guess one of the main jobs we have to do is getting the Sunday room ready for them," Mother interjected as she continued to organize preparations in her head. "It hasn't been used for awhile, so it will need a good cleanin' and dustin'."

After the high tide of excitement had passed, we drifted back to our previous occupations and activities.

By afternoon I prepared to fulfill my pledge to read the Bible and to continue my preparations for becoming a missionary. So with Mother's Bible and my latest romance, "The Story of Waitstill Baxter" by Kate Douglas Wiggins (by now I had completed "Freckles"), I slipped upstairs to the privacy of our bedroom since the day was pleasant enough to make this spot comfortable. I sat on the floor with the bed as a back prop and dutifully opened the Bible for my first assignment. I struggled through a few of the Genesis chapters, often with some perplexity. Where were all the exciting Old Testament stories that we had been taught in Sunday School? I struggled on, "What in the world does 'begat' mean? Begat, begat, begat, begat, begat, over and over. The person who wrote that sure didn't know many words, else he wouldn't use the same one so often."

Finally I decided to skip the begats and go to the end of the chapter. "I can't ever remember all those names and I can't pronounce them either," I thought. Unaware of it, I was rationalizing my way through the Old Testament.

As I was wont to do, I laid the Bible aside and was soon engrossed in "The Story of Waitstill Baxter."

In the days that followed, along with the regular farm tasks, we were making preparations for Grace's arrival. When the time came for bread baking and butter making, it occurred to me that perhaps I could strike a bargain with Mother—I should have known better. I rather enjoyed the bread making process: plunging both my hands in the mixture of flour, shortening, home-brewed yeast, and salt, forming it into a massive lump of soft spongy dough, and finally shaping it into loaves. However, I didn't like turning that churn handle round and round to make the butter come. So I approached Mother with a proposition, "I'll make the bread if Frances will do the churnin'."

Mother looked at me and calmly said, "Esther, you can make the bread if you want to, that will help. But you'll still have to help Frances with the churnin'. That's too much for her to do alone."

This ploy didn't work out as I had planned. Now I had two tasks to perform instead of one.

Bertha was ready to clean the Sunday Room for Grace's and Doctor's occupancy. "Come on, Esther, you can help me upstairs."

I was ready and willing, almost eager, to do her bidding, for we didn't often go to this room; it was usually kept closed with the shades drawn except when we were expecting over-night company.

Its contents consisted of a marble topped dresser with its tall slim mirror, a wash bowl and pitcher, a toothbrush holder and soap dish, each decorated with a fullblown pink rose on the side. Behind the washstand a back splash embroidered with red thread spelled out a "Splash! Splash!"

We, mostly Bertha, washed the windows, swept the floor and dusted the furniture. We stretched sheets over the little used straw tick that was still a well-rounded fat blimp. "I wish my tick was still big and high like that, but the straw is so broken up and mashed down that I can feel our bed ropes through it sometimes," I remarked.

"Well it won't be too long before threshing time. I guess then we can fill our ticks with new straw. Then you and Frances can have some fun for awhile. Just so you stay off our bed. I don't want any more jumpin' on it and knockin' down the slats like you did last year," Bertha cautioned.

While we chatted we finished making up the bed by spreading one of Mother's handloomed counterpanes over it.

Mother's special shams covered the pillows which we propped against the head board. On them were fat little cherubs embroidered in red, with the inscriptions: "Angels sing thee to sleep" on one, and "Angels guard thy slumber" on the other. How lovely they were!

The visit of Grace and her family was a happy, pleasant interlude in our farm routine. From the moment they arrived at the train station in Staunton and were brought home, Jesse, the first new generation member in our family was adored by two grandparents, four uncles and six doting aunts.

Anytime Frances and I could tow him in we introduced him to the numerous facets of the Pence estate andinstructed him in the rules and routines of running a farm:

—from the orchard where we picked up apples, "Don't pick up the rotton apples, Jesse, they aren't worth anything. Be sure to pick up only the good ones, Grandmother wants them to cook."

"Don't mess around the bees. They might sting you and that really hurts."

—to the chicken house where we gathered eggs, "Don't mess with the old settin' hens. They might pick you. They get real cross sometimes."

"Be careful with that egg. Put it in the basket real easy or you will break it."

"Watch where you step in here."

—to the woodpile where we picked up cobs and chips, "Help us pick up the chips, Jesse. Grandmother uses them to start fires in the mornings."

"Not the big pieces of wood, just the small ones!"

"Hey, don't throw the cobs at the chickens like that! It isn't good to scare them."

Each day we squeezed a few more potatoes and beans in the pot, we plucked and shucked more ears of corn, and always we sliced extra cucumbers and tomatoes. The hours were busy and bright and full of merriment.

We sat shoulder to shoulder around the long rectangular family table, which didn't even allow for a fraction of space for maneuvering to shove and push each other. There could only be frequent verbal battles. Jesse sat by his mother on a Sears Roebuck catalog, at least for the time being. Hopefully, the present one in the outhouse would outlast their visit, it had not yet been torn over to the farm machinery pages (we were now in the men's wear department). Our house was staunch and stout and withstood the vigorous assaults of walking and running, skipping and jumping; though there must have been times when it felt weary and old.

The most noteworthy event to take place during their visit was soon planned for and carried through. One day at the dinner table Mother announced to the family, "Your Pappy and I have decided that while Grace and Charlie are here we are going to town and have a family picture made. It is so hard to get us all together with Grace so far away, so we'll do it while we can."

"Yes, and as the years pass and all of you get older it will become harder and harder," added Pappy.

"Oh boy, we'll get to go to Harrisonburg once again!"

"Gee! That sounds like fun!"

"When will we go?"

"We thought we'd have an early dinner on Monday and leave right afterwards. I think I'd better call Mr. Dean, the photographer, and make an appointment for that time," Pappy replied.

"Do you reckon Mr. Dean will have a big enough camera to get us all in it?"

Pappy laughed, "I don't think you need to worry about that."

"Are you afraid you'll bust the camera?" Charlie teased.

"How will we all get to Harrisonburg? We sure can't all ride in one car."

"One of the Smith boys will drive some of us in their car. Several will have to start early and go in the buggy," Pappy explained.

"What will we wear?"

"You girls will wear your Sunday dresses and the boys their good suits. We'll want to look our best," Mother said.

We spent some time the next few days making sure everyone's best clothes were clean and pressed and all shoes were polished. Of necessity, the schedule of baths in the tin wash tub began early on Saturday afternoon—sufficient for Monday.

While this process was going on, Wilbur and Jake, unknown to the rest of the family, disappeared and then reappeared about an hour later. As they walked into the kitchen door Mother glanced up. The pan in her hand clattered to the floor. She was aghast when she beheld them.

"Boys! What in the world have you gone and done to your heads?"

What the boys had done, to Mother's dismay and chagrin, was to walk down to Edwin's and have him clip their hair with a pair of sheep clippers as short and as close to their heads as possible. And just two days before the sitting for the family portrait!

Mother, who was usually so calm and serene, was at the point of losing her composure. In exasperation she scolded, "I just can't understand why you boys would do a thing like this! You'll be a sight to have your pictures taken! You look about as bare as two peeled onions!"

"Well there's nothing we can do now. We can't make your hair grow back," she said at last, resignedly.

"We just thought it would be cooler this way; we never thought about takin' the picture," they explained meekly.

This meekness or feeble explanation didn't save them from the disdain of the rest of the family through the evening hours.

"Who ran a mower over you?"

"Cabbage heads!"

"How could you do such a thing?"

"You look like two picked pullets!" followed them around until they scurried off to bed before they were told to go.

No further major mishap or blunder occurred from that time until Monday, when we managed to get the convoy of assorted vehicles loaded, on the road, and to Harrisonburg. And we managed also to get all thirteen to Mr. Dean's studio and arranged in a satisfactory pose, without any damage to him or his equipment.

In spite of the two clipped heads, Mother and Pappy treasured this picture of their big family and the children still cherish it today. (Wilbur and Jake really looked kinda' cute, we had to admit).

Matters, Religious and Otherwise

After Grace's departure we drifted back into normal farm living, sooner than we would have chosen to. We were confronted with the many farm tasks associated with this time of year.

In today's technological world much of this work would be considered mundane and laborious. We must confess that we, too, oftimes found our work to be drudgery and not always challenging and interesting; but necessary for sustaining the family. Also, perhaps unconsciously, we were developing work habits and a work ethic that our parents, at least, must have considered valuable.

We began by joggling to the new ground over the up and down wagon road on a bright warm morning to harvest our year's potato crop. Here Jake, Frances and I followed Jasper's plow as it split open the soft brown earth, rolling out buckets of potatoes on either side of the furrow. Our rough brown feet plodded along behind the plow, our busy hands filling our containers as we went.

We almost daily schnitzed apples to dry for sale, for family use and for apple butter boiling. We dried corn and cut and stomped cabbage into sauerkraut.

We later went back to the same new ground, in the same big wagon, over the same bumpy road, to pull up the dried bunch beans. We loaded them in the wagon, and on our return, unloaded them onto the barn floor. The family had a full afternoon's project in pulling the pods off the vines and shelling and winnowing the beans.

Events occurred other than daily work which were also important to the life of our family and community. Mother was a member of the Sisters' Aid Society which met monthly and planned ways in which they could be useful to the church. In August they were scheduled to meet at our house. Now that I was trying to take my future and my Christian commitment more seriously I was delighted. These Sisters came mostly driving their buggies and horses. They were garbed rather simply in long dresses that were modest and unrevealing. Their long hair was brushed neatly back from their faces and tucked in buns at the tops or backs of their heads. And on each head was a white bobbinet prayer covering which was essential to a woman at any church gathering. They lined our parlor on the stiff, straight, uncomfortable chairs.

Mother had given me permission to be present at the meeting, provided I sat still and didn't talk; so here I was now perched on a stool at her side, face, hands and bare feet scrubbed clean, and with wide eyes and open ears.

Aunt Betty Harshbarger was president of the group, and as she prepared to open the meeting she turned to a member and asked, "Sister Ida, will you lead us in an opening hymn?"

From Greenland's icy mountains,
From India's coral strand,
Where Africa's sunny fountains
Roll down their golden sands,
From many an ancient river
From many a palmy plain,
They call us to deliver
Their land from error's chain.

Can we whose souls are lighted
By wisdom from on high,
Can we to men benighted
The lamp of light deny?
Salvation, O salvation!
The joyful sound proclaim,
Till earth's remotest nation
Has learned Messiah's name.

I was so glad they sang a missionary hymn and almost wondered if they were singing it to me. I had no idea what "coral strand" or "error's chain" meant, but they were pretty sounding words, I thought. I was "bustin" to say to Mother, "I think that song was about Africa"; however, I remembered her words of caution before the meeting and kept my thoughts within.

I tried to listen intently as the meeting proceeded through: the roll call, the reading of the minutes, the business items.

I was impressed by the minutes that recorded some of their activities:

Sister Cline was appointed to make two black aprons for baptism. The goods cost forty three cents.

It was moved and seconded that any lady of good moral character may become a member of the Society with the understanding that the controls be kept under the Church of the Brethren.

Six gingham suits were made and donated to the children in the orphan's home at Timberville.

We decided to donate two of our comforts to Bridgewater College.

Five dollars was sent to the support of our India orphan.

We furnished the Morris family, who was about burned out by the fire, with two of our comforts and two bed ticks. Many of our ladies gave needed items out of their own supplies.

New business:

"I brought ten bleached sugar pokes along with me for making our 'counterpins.' I also brought a coupla' spools of turkey red silkateen thread so we can put them together with briar stitch."

"I think we have about enough pokes so that we can have a sewing day soon. We'll be needing to think about a time for that."

"Our contribution for the support of Brother Isaac and Sister Effie Long is about due. The Church has been given some mighty good reports about the great work they are doing in India."

("Maybe some day my church will support me on some mission field just like they are doing now for Cousin Ike and Cousin Effie," I thought.)

"I have something I'd like to bring up. We all know Aunt Patty Mac and how much she has helped so many of our families. She has performed as midwife for births in our community and helped others after the babies come. She doesn't have a husband or family to provide for her like the most of us. Now she is old and had to have all her teeth pulled, but doesn't have money to buy a set of false ones. Do you reckon we could pay for a set for her? I believe they cost around five dollars. She can hardly eat anything and it makes a body feel real bad to see her in such a shape."

(As they discussed this I was so glad they decided to help Aunt Patty, 'cause I remembered that Aunt Mary couldn't eat corn off the cob when she visited us while Grace was home. Mother had to cut it off for her.)

"A committee was appointed to ask the elders of the church if they would have any objections to the society putting a cushion on their bench at the church. Sister Maggie do you have a report on this yet?"

"Yes, I talked to a coupla' them and they felt God would not look kindly upon the elders accepting greater comforts than their brethren, but they wished to express their appreciation for the sisters' kindness in this."

"I think we need to respect our elders in this matter and we ought to appreciate the humility they demonstrate to us."

("Our preachers are such good men," I thought.)

"Some of our sisters have been talking that maybe it's time to think about making our caps a different way. Some of our churches are making round pleated caps. They are so much easier to make."

"Yes, I've heard, too, that some sisters from other churches are beginning to use these round caps. But it seems to me that we ought to be pretty careful in laying aside our practices and moving into such worldly ways. You know our founders believed that we should be separate and apart in our dress and the way we live, and according to the scripture 'we should not be conformed to this world.' "

"We all know that St. Paul said a woman should pray with her head covered, but he didn't say what the covering had to look like or what shape it had to be. The round ones would save us time and goods, so we could sell them cheaper."

"Saving goods is not important. If we keep trying to save goods, pretty soon they'll get so small they won't be any bigger than my hand."

"Well, I for one don't mind making them as they are now. If we begin to break away from our present ways, pretty soon we'll be wanting to wear earrings and such like."

"It seems that we have different feelings among our sisters on this. Maybe we'd better put the decision off until next meeting. In the meantime let's all pray about it and seek the guidance of the Holy Spirit."

"Today is the day for our egg offering."

"I'll give the price of two dozen eggs."

"And I'll give the price of two dozen eggs."

"I'll give the price of one dozen eggs. Our old hens have just about quit layin'."

"I'll give the price of a hen."

("The price of an ole' hen! Gee! Mother, isn't that a lot for one person to give?" I whispered in Mother's ear, so startled by what seemed to me to be such great generosity that I forgot I was supposed to keep silent.)

Mother whispered back, "Yes, but she is able to give more than some of the rest of us."

"Sister Ida will you lead us in one verse of 'God be with You 'Til We Meet Again,' after which we will say together the Lord's Prayer."

As all the Sisters knelt in prayer by their chairs I knelt with them and felt very noble and committed at this moment.

Come Sunday, and it was Pappy's preaching appointment time at Baugher's Chapel. Mill Creek, being a rather large self-sustaining congregation, supported several mission points at some distance, yet within the orbit of the church. Our Pappy was a part of the free ministry that shepherded the flock in the early years of the coming of the Brethren to our community. Those participating in this ministry at Mill Creek usually took turns preaching in these somewhat isolated small churches. Baugher's Chapel, one of these several preaching points, was located a bit north and east of the town of Elkton and in the foothills of the Blue Ridge Mountains. In those days this seemed quite a distance to travel.

Since the services were to be in the afternoon, Mother decided it might be nice for Frances and me and herself to accompany Pappy. Pappy thought that would be nice also. Jasper would be our chauffeur.

"Girls, how would you like to pack a picnic dinner Sunday and go to Bear Lithia Springs to eat, then go over to Baugher's Chapel in the afternoon where your Pappy has to preach?" Mother asked us.

"Oh boy! That sounds like fun!" was my excited reply.

"Let's do! Let's do! I like picnics!" Frances exclaimed, just as joyously.

"What can we have to eat on our picnic?" I inquired.

"Let's have fried chicken! I'd like to have a chicken leg!" suggested Frances.

"Ham is good too," I added. "And I also like chicken. I could eat either one."

"I don't know yet what we will have, but we'll fix something you like," promised Mother.

If you were to ask, "Whoever heard of a picnic without either hotdogs or hamburgers?" my reply to you would be that we never knew of a picnic with hotdogs and hamburgers.

Sunday dawned vivid and clear after a miniature shower on Saturday—just perfect for an outing. Thus, at leaving time we were ready to go. Frances and I were dressed in our Sunday best. Mother, too, with her good bonnet, under which was her white bobbinet prayer covering with its narrow black ribbons tied under her chin. Jasper wore a suit, a tie, and a dress shirt; we seldom saw Jasper in this formal attire, except on Sundays. Pappy was clothed in the Brethren's regular black buttoned-up coat with its celluloid collar rimming the neck and, of course, the usual long black trousers, black shoes, and black hat. For a man who was as handsome as my Pappy, that was a very drab garb indeed. We considered church to be important, whether it was a plain little wooden one located along a stream up some hollow in the Blue Ridge Mountains or a brick stained glass windowed one in the city of Harrisonburg.

With Jasper at the wheel and Pappy beside him in the front seat, and Mother, Frances, and me and the dinner basket in the back, we rattled and rocked along in our Maxwell over the once wintry rutty roads now crumpled into summer's dust. Where were all the allergies that should have plagued us then? I surmise they were unknown. When we left the cross country roads and turned onto the Spotswood Trail we headed east toward the Blue Ridge Mountains.

Pappy, who always had a sense of history, took the opportunity to again teach Frances and me a history lesson. He began, "A long time ago Virginia had a governor named Alexander Spotswood. Governor Spotswood wanted to see what was on this side of the mountain, so he and a group of men left the Capitol at Williamsburg and started out, riding horseback much of the time. Some days later, after many hardships, they reached the top of the mountain that is just ahead of us. As they stood at the top of this ridge they could see the end of the Massanutten Mountain just over there to our left and had a clear view all the way across the valley to the Alleghenies in the west. Governor Spotswood and his men came on down into the valley, and their trail was just about where this road is now. So they called it 'Spotswood Trail,' naming it for the governor. As a reward he gave each of his men a little golden horseshoe, and ever after that he called them 'Knights of the Golden Horseshoe.' "

"That was a real good story, Pappy," I said and then asked, "Where did the name Shenandoah come from?"

"Shenandoah is a beautiful name given to our valley by the Indians and it means 'Daughter of the Stars,' " he answered, supplying me with another bit of history.

Not long thereafter something went "psss-ss-st" then "bump"!

"Oh, oh, we have a flat tire," Jasper said, pulling off to the side of the road and stopping. He removed his coat and rolled up his sleeves, readying himself for the job to be done. Frances, Mother and Pappy, and I stood beside the road to watch, useless excess baggage at the moment.

Jasper pulled up the back seat and, reaching in the space below, took out the jack, the inner tube patching material, the tire irons, and the air pump. He jacked up the rear end of the car by placing the jack under the axle. With the irons he pried the tire off the rim. Removing the tube from the casing, he made a visual inspection to find the hole, with no success. Thus, he partially inflated it, and held it to his ear to locate the spot where the air was escaping. Finally succeeding, he marked the spot, let the air out and proceeded to do the patching job. First, he spread the tube on the front fender for a flat surface, then scratched the surface around the hole to roughen it and make the patch adhere. Next he applied glue to this area, cut a patch the desired size, then after the glue had dried slightly, he placed on the patch and applied pressure to it. He checked the tire to see if he could find the tack or nail that had caused the flat and removed the offensive weapon. At last he put the tube back in the tire, and with the use of the irons forced it back on the rim, inflated the tire again, and jacked down instead of up.

Finally, Jasper went to the front of the car to start the motor; grasping the crank he gave it a vigorous upward pull. The engine sputtered a time or two then misfired.

"Twist its tail again, Jasper!" I called, mimicking the menfolk of the family.

Jasper ignored me, but did just that. This time the engine sputtered and coughed a time or two, then took off. Our Maxwell shuddered and shook, but the engine continued to putt-putt.

At length, we fitted ourselves back together again and were on our way—but not for long. A few miles down the road and again that unwelcome sound, "Psss-ss-st!"

"Not again!" I wailed looking over the side of the car when Jasper pulled to the side of the road.

As Jasper went through the whole procedure once more we were beginning to wonder if we could ever have our dinner and get to the church on time.

Fortunately, that was our last flat tire and we did arrive at Bear Lithia Springs not too long thereafter, hungry, thirsty, dusty and tired.

The clear, cool, bubbling spring was a refreshing sight. We drank with relish the water, that maintains a 52 degree temperature, until our thirst was quenched. With the eager assistance of Frances and me, Mother began to unpack the food basket, at least until the chicken platter was revealed. Chicken legs never looked so enticing nor ever tasted better. We attacked them, along with a piece of butter bread, before we scarcely inspected the rest of the food. Mother set out hard boiled eggs homemade pickles, potato salad, and apple pie. And of course there was all the cool, fresh, unpolluted, spring water we could drink—for free. Everyone was famished enough that everything soon disappeared, and Mother concluded the meal by saying, "I'm glad we got shut of all the food. It wouldn't be so good to leave it settin' around in the hot car all afternoon."

As she gathered things together Frances and I strolled around the rock wall that encircled this large spring, now and then pausing to gaze into its clear bubbling depths, until Pappy called "Come on, daughters, we must get on our way now or we'll be late to church."

We collected ourselves in the car again and prayerfully started on our way, hoping for no more ominous sounds from one of the tires.

We arrived at the little church in the woods with a sense of relief, walked inside, and found our seats preparatory to the services of the afternoon.

A dozen or more women, several leading barefooted children by their hands, filed into the church behind us. They were followed by their men with shirt collars open and sleeves rolled up, for it was a rather warm afternoon. The windows were open wide to let in the little breeze that stirred the leaves on the trees ever so slightly.

The program for the service was a typical one; opening hymn, scripture and prayer. Then our Pappy took his place behind the crude pulpit and delivered his exhortation about sin, repentance and salvation. His powerful resonant voice filled every nook and cranny of the small church and took flight through the open windows, perhaps to reach the ears of some entrepreneur in a mountian hollow operating his still.

Flies and bees buzzed in and out the open windows unchallenged as the service droned on.

As he concluded his sermon with the same vigor he had introduced it, Pappy pulled his handkerchief from his pants pocket and mopped the perspiration from his moist face. Then he addressed one of the audience, "Mr. Morris, will you lead us in a closing hymn?"

Mr. Morris had a florid rotund face and a full chest that extended from his neck to the terminus of his abdomen. His stout arms were flung across the back of his seat, giving impetus to this expansiveness.

In response to Pappy's request, he started to sing without any further announcement and in a voice that boomed forth so loudly I was quite startled; hence, I turned and stared at him in fascination as he began:

When the trum - pet of the Lord
shall sound and time shall be no more;
And the morn - ing breaks e - ter - nal
bright and fair.
When the saints of earth shall gath - er
o - ver on the oth - er shore,
And the roll is called up yon - der
I'll be there.

When the roll is called up yon - der
When the roll is called up yon - der
When the roll is called up yon - der
When the roll is called up yon - der
I'll be there.

As I listened raptly, I reckoned that he was pretty tired and hot since the afternoon was so warm and he didn't feel much like singing. He seemed to stop, not just between each word, but between each syllable.

Mr. Morris appeared to be in no hurry to leave this life, but I wondered if the roll might not be called up yonder before he finished the song.

The trip home was uneventful, much to the relief of each passenger in our unpredictable Maxwell.

In those early days an event that was almost as constant as the cycle of the seasons that ushered in autumn and certain farm chores was the holding of revival services. This was true of most churches, be they large or small. The little Methodist church that sat within gossiping range of Timber Ridge School fell into this category. And since it was a happening within our walking orbit we wanted to be present—at least occasionally. There weren't many events of good repute in the community that we didn't attend, participate in, or observe. We went for the most part because we enjoyed the opportunities to get together with friends and acquaintances around us. We did not attend a revival meeting because we felt a need for repentance, forgiveness and conversion. Most of us had already joined the church and in our own childish naive way we thought everything had been taken care of, that we were assured of salvation when we made our confession and were baptized. How little we knew! We were unaware of the number of times we would be sorely tried and tested, or how often we would be tempted and fall from grace. In our own naiveté we did not yet know that each day of our lives we would need to experience rebirth and renewal in our search for God's will and fullness of life.

And so it was when the news was spread about that the "big meetin' " was starting at Timber Ridge, it was just assumed that we Pence children would attend, along with the Bowmans and Frances D.

The first several nights of the meeting started off rather mildly and routinely, beginning with a rather lengthy song service, followed by the minister's scripture reading and prayer, the sermon, and the closing hymn and benediction.

Some young neighborhood boys stood outside, occasionally peering through the open windows with frivolous curiousity or perhaps to spot a girl that they might like to drive home in their buggies, or if they were without these accouterments, to walk her home.

By the middle of the week the tenor of the meeting grew in intensity as the minister began warming up to his mission and the call for the unchurched. With evangelical fervor he hurled his denunciations of sin and evil at his audience, consigning the sinner to damnation, destruction, and eternal hellfire.

"Amen!" ardently affirmed a bearded elderly man on the deacon's bench skirting the right side of the pulpit.

The evangelist seemed to have only two volumes, louder and loudest, until near the close of his discourse his voice was squeezed into a hoarse raspy sound that was barely audible. He moved and bobbed and swayed, shaking his fists at no one in particular but at everyone in general. After he felt that he had sufficiently put the fear of God in his congregation, he began pleading, "Repent of your sins and come to Jesus while there is yet time."

"Amen! Amen!"

"As we sing the invitation hymn, 'Why Not Tonight?' won't you come forward and give me your hand and your heart to God? Tomorrow may be too late, for we know not what day or at what hour God's hand will strike."

"Amen!"

> Oh, do not let the word depart,
> And close thine eyes against the light;
> Poor sinner, harden not your heart;
> Be saved, oh, tonight.
>
> Oh, why not tonight?
> Oh, why not tonight?
> Wilt thou be saved?
> Then why not tonight?

As I curiously turned and looked over the audience, I observed a certain restlessness among the crowd and I kept hoping someone would come forward and answer the preacher's call.

By now the minister's wife was moving up and down the aisles searching for the unsaved, "Are you a Christian? Won't you come forward and confess your sins tonight before it's too late?"

> Only trust Him, only trust Him,
> Only trust Him now.
> He will save you, He will save you,
> He will save you now.

One young girl slowly made her way up the aisle as the preacher greeted her with outstretched hands, "God bless you, my child."

Then turning to his congregation, he said, "I think the spirit is beginning to move among us. Won't you come now while we sing the next hymn? If you don't want to come forward, stand where you are until you are recognized."

> Come home, come home,
> Ye who are weary, come home;
> Earnestly, tenderly, Jesus is calling,
> Calling, O sinner, come home!

By now the minister's wife had reached the pew where our group sat, Bertha at the end near the aisle. Putting her hand on

Bertha's startled shoulder, she asked, "Are you a Christian?"

Bertha replied with her usual candor, "I try to be."

"Tryin' to be and bein' ain't the same thing!" she said sternly, whipping Bertha with her foreboding words as she moved on to the next prospective sinner.

Almost persuaded, harvest is past!
Almost persuaded, dawn comes at last!
Almost cannot avail,
Almost is but to fail!
Sad, sad, that bitter wail,
Almost, but lost.

Finally, when the meeting ended we stepped outside into the refreshing night air, away from the stuffiness of the little church and the heat generated by the emotionally charged bodies.

As we walked along briskly toward home, any twinges of conscience that we may have felt during the meeting dissipated as rapidly, as our feet rose and fell in the dust of the road. By the time we had reached the Johnson house. a short distance from the church, we were completely conscienceless, for it was at this spot that our propensity for making mischief took over. Here lived a woman who seemed to have little appreciation for the rollicking high spirits of youngsters—or perhaps we had little respect for the low melancholy spirits of this elderly woman. Whichever way it was, the situation presented a challenge to a group of fun-loving, mischief-making young people. From past similar occasions we knew it would take very little to arouse her ire; we had experienced this on certain evenings when we had passed by on our way home from school.

As was usual, Frances D. was the instigator of such capers, although this is not to excuse the rest of us for our willing participation in such activities.

When we neared the house we could see only the shadowy farm buildings in the darkness. Frances began giggling and prodded, "Hey! Let's see if we can't get Mrs. Johnson stirred up. I bet she'd really get mad this time a night."

We were all too willing partners in crime; we began laughing raucously and started singing,

Oh, it ain't gonna' rain no more, no more,
It ain't gonna' rain no more.
How in the heck can I wash my neck

If tain't gonna' rain no more?

"Fools! Fools! Fools!" These words shot out from somewhere in the blackness.

Then more laughter on our parts.

"A lotta' good it did you to go to church tonight and then come out and carry on like a bunch of fools!" (This seemed to be her favorite epithet).

"Maybe you oughta' try goin' to church once," somebody shouted back.

"Yeh!"

"Yeh!"

"Yeh!" came the agreement from the group, warming up to the situation.

Mrs. Johnson hurled another broadside at us, "Didn't do you no good to go!" Then raved on, "That ole' Miz' Showalter won't go to the table without slappin' somethin' on her head and look how she raised that Frances Diehl! And that Sam Pence gits up in the pulpit on Sunday and preaches everbody in his church to heaven, and look at his younguns! They're on the wrong road! They're goin' straight to hell!"

More giggling.

"Now git yourselves outa' here! 'Cause if the devil don't git you I will!"

As her rage reached this degree of intensity we were in truth beginning to feel a little frightened; perhaps we had carried things a bit too far. Ruth, sensing this, took over, "Come on you all, let's get on home before anything happens and we really get into trouble."

At this welcome suggestion we hastened our steps. As we moved along our talking and laughing were a bit more subdued, for at that point we truly were a little stunned at the violent reactions of this bitter woman.

Arriving home, we crawled into bed with the strange mixture of old time religion, mischief, guilt, fear and contrition in our heads. Those thoughts may not have been compatible, but if so they did not prevent us from falling asleep almost immediately. However, for the entire first week of school we avoided passing the Johnson place by climbing the fences and cutting across Saufley's fields and from thence to the Crossroads, where we parted company with our friends.

The closing of revival meeting signaled the opening of school. Ruth and Bertha packed their trunks and were soon off to Bridgewater Academy. Elizabeth returned to her classroom, and Charlie to his work at B. Ney's Store. No matter how large the family or how frequent the departure, there is always a sense of loss, thus the leave-taking left quite a void in our home. When this happens there is always involved a shifting and reassigning of many functions and tasks. But soon the rest of us fell into the routine of school and performance of farm and household chores, minus the four non-resident ones.

By the time school opened, I discovered my text books more enticing and inspiring to read and more on my understanding level—thus my Bible study fell somewhere between the begators and the begatees and between the kings and the kingdoms.

Each progression in grades brought new and challenging subjects to learn. This year I was introduced to the continent of Africa in our study of geography. We not only learned about its political divisions, its climate, its mountains and its deserts, but we were introduced to its animal and plant life. That was the beginning of my undoing. We were thoroughly immersed in the study of the jungles and streams inhabited by crocodiles, huge snakes, gorillas and hippopotamuses, and on the plains fierce lions and leopards and enormous elephants. For many of my classmates this was the most interesting and thrilling part of geography. For me it presented a foreboding picture of Africa; India wasn't much better with its tigers and snakes. After a few days in this part of the study my resolve to be a missionary began to waiver. Being romantic, I had overlooked my fears of snakes and wild animals and man-eating savages. Finally, this ambition, this dream, too passed—if I weren't ready to take my wings and fly to Hollywood, neither was I ready to take a boat and sail to "Darkest Africa" or "Idol-worshiping India."

Rich man, poor man,
Beggar man, thief.
Doctor, lawyer,
Indian chief.

Housewife, teacher,
. . . . Missionary afar
Nurse, "glad girl",
. . . .

I had lost another button.

PART THREE: THE YEAR OF POLLYANNA

Spring and An Easter Tradition

Country children know when spring arrives, not only by the return of warm days and no coat weather, but by many other signs that manifest themselves on the farm with the advent of this season—and by certain less visible indications known only to those who experience them (shedding long underwear and heavy black stockings).

Spring had arrived, there was no doubt about it. Along the creeks and down through the hollows the greening willows were sweeping the sky in the gentle spring breeze.

In the grove along the road to school we saw two brown bunnies "twitterpating" among the pines.

As we reached the Crossroads we tarried longer under the ancient timeworn cedar tree, reluctant to part company. Those arriving first confiscated the plank bench placed across the exposed roots where the soil had crumbled away from them as they clung to the bank in one angle of the Crossroads.

New hommys (calves) were nursing the mother cows and trying their wobbly legs in the field fronting our farm house.

Nearby, the buds on the apple trees in Pappy's orchard were splitting their jackets, displaying their pinkness and fragrance.

As we entered the yard gate we beheld Mother's Easter flowers parading around the white paling fence that squared our front yard.

At dusk the frogs in the meadow emerged from their mud beds to serenade us with a slightly dissonant spring concert.

As the days grew warmer our long underwear became more itchy, the worn button holes bigger so that the flaps flapped more than ever. We knew, however, the time was approaching when we could shed this apparel, along with our exhausted shoes.

We were now gathering our supply of iron in the forms of dandelion and dry land cress in the fields around us.

Our store of foods: fruits, dried corn, dried beans was disappearing, but we never seemed to run out of apple butter—it was always there.

With the advent of warm weather, potatoes in the cellar were sprouting and shriveling, thus we were constantly desprouting and peeling wrinkled ones.

Each morning an old red rooster flew to the top of the wood pile, held his head high, flapped his wings and crowed, "Cock-a-doodle-doo," as if to say, "Those baby chicks in that coop in the chicken yard are my family; I am the father."

Easter was a special part of spring time on the Pence farm, as well as many other Dutch farms in the Valley. Along with the religious significance, we celebrated this holiday in secular ways. As far back as I could remember we had hidden eggs at Easter time, just like Mother did when she was a little girl, and Grossmommy and Grosspappy had done before her. "I suppose it's an old Dutch custom from the Old Country," Mother said.

Each year about a week before Easter we began confiscating eggs from the hens' nests and hiding them in the most obscure places we could find. It would add to the fun and excitement if one could discover another's cache and add them to one's own collection. Early on Easter Sunday morning the eggs would be brought to the house and proudly displayed before the family.

At the supper table, Jake, swallowing a mouthful of fried potatoes, blurted out, "I know where I'm gonna' hide my eggs this year and I don't want anybody stealin' 'em."

And Wilbur added, "I betcha' nobody is gonna' find mine 'cause I've thought up a real good place."

"Maybe all of us will have a better chance to keep our eggs hidden since Bertha and Ruth aren't here to sneak 'em," I suggested.

Mary glanced slyly around the table saying nothing. No doubt she was thinking, "I'll be the oldest this year, so I'll be able to take their place and sneak eggs like they did."

I thought Pappy looked a little sly himself as he watched and listened. He truly was our nemesis, for he was the best sleuth in the business, somehow usually fereting out where all the caches were.

Each evening as I gathered the eggs, first in the hen house and then in the barn, I made my plans and proceeded to carry them out. I set my basket down on the barn floor, walked to the big sliding doors and cast a sharp eye in all directions. I stepped back and listened for approaching footsteps within. At last satisfied that all was well, I took some eggs from the basket and hid them in what I believed was an undiscoverable place, then carefully camouflaged any telltale signs. After I was satisfied that no one was aware of my maneuvering, I picked up my basket and walked nonchalantly to the house. This gradually became my daily routine.

The week was an exciting one, much running hither and thither, eggs coming and going, appearing, disappearing, reappearing. Youngsters spying and sneaking, hiding and rehiding. And somehow Pappy always in the barkground knowing what his sons and daughters were up to.

On Easter morning by the time the sun peeped over the Blue Ridge to the east, I awoke, my flesh tingling with excitement. I heard Pappy rattling the stove lids below, preparing to start the fire for Mother to cook breakfast. A bit later he came to the foot of the stairs and called, "Children, get up! It's time to get your work done before church! Get up right away! Boys! Jasper, Wilbur, Jake! Girl's! Mary, Esther, Frances!"

After some dawdling and scrambling everyone was finally downstairs.

In a few minutes Wilbur and Jake appeared in the doorway each carrying a small number of eggs.

"My eggs kept disappearin' so I had to keep changin' my hidin' place and this is all I have left," said Wilbur displaying three eggs.

"Same thing here," added Jake. "I bet nobody is gonna' find my hidin' place next year, I betcha'."

"Oh yeah?" teased Mary. She was not very sympathetic to Jake's probelm, for just last evening Pappy had discovered her eggs in the old buggy behind the chicken house. The boys had thought that was funny and now it was her time to laugh.

While this conversation was taking place I slipped quietly into the pantry, picked up the egg basket and walked quickly to the barn. I carefully lifted all the lovely brown eggs from my hiding place and laid them in the basket. Mother and Pappy had taught us to handle the eggs with care. None must be broken, for many of them would be traded at the store for such necessary items as shoes, long underwear, sugar, spices, coal oil for the lamps.

I retraced my steps to the house, and as I entered the kitchen I heard Mary ask, "Where's Esther?"

"Here I am!" I shouted. "And look at all my eggs!"

"Gee whiz! Look at all those eggs!" Wilbur yelled.

"Where have you been hidin' them?" Mary asked, her eyes popping.

"Yeah, I'd like to know, too. Tell us, Esther," begged Jake.

"Daughter, it looks as if you outwitted your old Pappy this time," he laughed.

"Come on, Esther, tell us where you hid them," cajoled Wilbur.

"No! No! No!" I answered vehemently. "I might wanna' use my place again next year. So I'm not gonna' tell you. Never, never, never!"

This was about my happiest Easter.

Pollyanna and the "Glad Game"

As this celebration moved into the past, school closing was moving rapidly into the present, but there could be no goofing off from studies or homework—our teachers saw to that. They would teach and give home assignments until our authoritative no-nonsense bell would signal the closing of school for the year.

We had to respond by doing the homework assigned to us without question or procrastination. So the final nights of school found us seated around the dinner table with our assortment of readers, arithmetics, histories, geographies, spellers, piled high in front of us. In the center of the table was the light by which we studied, an old-fashioned coal oil lamp.

At the bottom of my stack of books could be found one that had no relation to school work. As soon as I had done my arithmetic problems, studied my spelling words, and read my geography lesson, which included answering the questions at the end of the assignment, I quietly slipped this alien book from the others and began to read.

My movements did not escape the sharp eyes of Mary, for almost immediately she called to Mother, who was sitting by the fireplace in the living room (the stove having been removed for the season), "Mother, Esther's not studyin'; she's readin' a book!"

"Esther, have you finished studyin' your lessons?" Mother inquired.

"Yes I have; I've done my arithmetic problems, I studied my spellin' and my geography lessons and I know the answers to all the questions. The teacher reviewed us on all the states and capitols today and I didn't miss any of them. I studied my history lesson at school when the sixth grade was havin' their grammar class."

"Well all right then. What are you readin' now?"

"I'm readin' 'Pollyanna.' It's such a good book. Frances D. loaned 'Pollyanna' and 'Pollyanna Grows Up' to me the other day. I'll soon be through with 'Pollyanna.' "

"Yes, they are good books. I read them when Bertha and Ruth borrowed them. But don't read too long. I think it's about time you children go to bed anyhow. Your Pappy and I are going to turn in before too long. Be sure to outen' the lamp before you go."

Pappy was already dozing in his chair by the fireplace, his glasses clinging lopsidedly to the end of his nose, his newspaper in a disheveled heap on his lap.

When school closed I had more time to devote to Pollyanna, the child of a minister with a meagre salary serving in a small mission church. I was very moved by the situation that prompted Pollyanna to begin playing the "Glad Game." This is the story as Pollyanna told it to Aunt Polly's maid, Nancy:

> It's called the 'just being glad game.' Father told it to me and it's lovely. We played it always, ever since I was a little, little girl. I told the Ladies Aid and they played it—some of them. We began it on some crutches that came in a missionary barrel. You see I wanted a doll, and Father had written so; but when the barrel came the lady wrote that there hadn't any dolls come in but the little crutches had. So she sent them along as they might come in handy for some child sometime. And that's when we began it. The game was to just find something about everything to be glad about—no matter what 'twas. And we began right then—on the crutches. At first I couldn't see anything to be glad about—getting a pair of crutches when you wanted a doll! Father had to tell me. He said just be glad you don't need 'em! You see it's just as easy when you know how!

The sadness I felt about Pollyanna was very real—my feelings were very vulnerable as those of youngsters often times are. I was just as passionate in my dislike for Aunt Polly, who had taken Pollyanna into her cold mansion to live when Pollyanna's missionary father died. Aunt Polly knew to do her duty by her niece, but she knew nothing at all about being glad. In this house Pollyanna found it difficult to honor her father's last request to play the "glad game". But the local doctor was soon using her as a tonic to his patients, especially the cross ones, and in a short time she brought happiness to the whole town with her sunny philosophy.

All the fairy tale boy-girl romance began when Pollyanna happened upon a runaway orphan boy along the road. And how she subsequently was able to persuade the wealthy recluse, John Pendleton, to adopt this orphan named Jimmy Bean.

In "Pollyanna Grows Up," as it so often happens to young readers, it was very difficult for me to separate my own dreams and fantasies from these two people as the friendship between them blossomed into love.

In the consistent routine of farm life during those years, a very special opportunity would occasionally come. This happened to me in the midst of my preoccupation with Pollyanna and the 'glad game.'

Bertha and Ruth came home from the Academy to spend a weekend with the family. The only thing I remember about that visit was the announcement they made, which was that the seniors at the College would be giving "Pollyanna" as their class play on the coming Saturday night.

"I wish . . ."

Before that aspiration was fully expressed, they asked Mother, "Could Esther spend the weekend with us so that she could see the play? She is so wrapped up in the book she'd probably really like it. It would be kinda' nice to have a little sister visit us, too."

I assailed my Mother with all the persuasive power with which I was endowed. "Can I, Mother, can I? Please let me go!" I begged. "Please! Please! I'll do everything you tell me to this week without fussin' once!"

Mother, bless her, didn't keep me in suspense long, "I don't see any reason why you can't go, if it suits Jasper to take you Saturday morning. I think it's real nice the girls want you to visit them and see the play."

"Hot dog! Wait 'til I tell Margaret and Elizabeth and Frances D. I can't wait 'til Saturday!" At the end of this outburst I dashed upstairs so that I could be sure to finish my book before the great day arrived.

But busy hands do not always busy minds make—that was an unpleasant reality I learned through the week that followed. My errant thoughts constantly drifted to the upcoming Saturday. No matter how much I longed for the time to pass, I could not shorten the days by one minute.

Frances and I played in our make-believe playhouse in the corner of the yard under the pear trees where I always pretended to be the sweet Pollyanna playing the 'glad game,' and Frances had to play the severe harsh Aunt Polly, not always to Frances' liking and certainly not true to her character. For sure, our playhouse in no way resembled Aunt Polly's mansion—it consisted of a plank laid across some bricks on which was our collection of thrown-away pieces of dishes, one broken-handled spoon and some discarded zinc can tops in which we made our mud pies. Do children make mud pies anymore? I wonder—with all the realistic toy ovens and the assortment of utensils and materials that are available. If not, then an entertaining and creative art has been lost.

One day, to Frances' and my delight, we found a hen that had stolen a nest, with her babies already beginning to hatch out. She had kept her nesting activities a secret in an obscure place, as hens with a strong mothering instinct often times do. As usual, Mother placed them in a box behind the stove to dry off. We hovered over the box, handling the little balls of down and fluff at every opportunity and as much as Mother would allow. It was pure joy to hold one quietly and gently between both palms 'til it slowly closed its little black beady eyes and went to sleep, then remove one hand while it remained unstirring and sleeping on the other. By evening, Mother decided it was time to place them in a coop with the anxious mother hen. She dabbed a bit of lard on the top of each baby's head, on both of their wings, and rubbed a bit on their little fuzzy behinds—to keep them from getting lice was the accepted reason for this preventive treatment.

On another day of this long week, when Margaret and Elizabeth came over to spend the afternoon, Wilbur and Jake cajoled us into riding down the barn hill in barrels again. I didn't much enjoy this stunt but it did help to pass the time away. Soon we tired of being bumped and jolted round and round. At that moment, Mary and Frances D. joined us and we agreed to play "Fox in the Morning." After counting, "Eerie, eirie, Acrie, Ann, . . . ," it was Wilbur's lot to be the fox. He stood behind our make-do base at the foot of the barn hill and we some fifty feet away near the windwheel.

He shouted, "Fox in the Morning!"

We shouted back, "Goose and the Gander!"

He called again, "How many comes out?"

Our answer, "More than you can manage!"

Then we all challenged him by running in his direction, hoping to get behind the base before he caught us. Any that were caught became foxes and were his assistants as we played the next round. We repeated this procedure until only one was left uncaught, who would then become the Fox to start the next game.

It really wasn't difficult to decide what I should wear for my weekend visit, since my wardrobe consisted of a couple of school dresses, an everyday dress or two and one Sunday dress suitable for this time of year; the latter of course would be the appropriate one. It was a gray jumper that Mother had made and which I had decorated with a running stitch of red wool thread around the neck and across the top of two big patch pockets. We washed and ironed the white blouse that went with it, and made sure that I had a clean petticoat, drawers, and my long black ribbed stockings. I washed and rubbed my black patent leather slippers, that had a strap that buttoned around the ankle, to a gloss that they had never known before—nor after. I washed my hair and took my Saturday night bath on Friday. On Saturday morning I packed my bag, a paper one containing a tooth brush and two clean handkerchiefs. After I had dressed with more than usual care, Mother combed my hair and topped it with a pretty red ribbon bow. Clutching my bag in one hand and my sweater in the other, I was ready to go.

Mother's parting words, "Now be a nice girl and listen to your sisters. Enjoy the play and you can tell the rest of us about it when you get back. Goodbye!"

"I will! I will!" to all her admonitions. "Goodbye!" as I dashed out the door to climb in the car with Jasper.

Being at college was an unexplored world to me, unknown and unfamiliar. A world with a tree shaded campus full of young men and women, dormitory life, dark-suited professors, one big dining hall where the students sat in groups around family-sized tables. Of course, as a little sister I enjoyed the attention and teasing I was getting from the fellows and girls.

But the most memorable part of my weekend was attending the presentation of the play. The story of Pollyanna that I had been reading now came alive, flesh and blood right before my eyes. Jimmy Bean, Aunt Polly, and Pollyanna became real people and a part of my existance; I rejoiced; I felt sadness; I was angered; finally, I felt contentment at the fairy tale ending—the rebirth of Aunt Polly and the "happiness ever after" for Pollyanna and Jimmy Bean.

Thoughts of the "glad game" lingered on after I returned home, and it was at this point I decided to be a Pollyanna too, find something to always be glad about, be "little miss sunshine," maybe to even find a Jimmy Bean and fall in love.

Acting out my fantasy began.

—Dinner time and Wilbur and Jake walked into the kitchen to wash up for dinner. Wilbur pulled off his straw hat, wiped the sweat off his forehead with his shirt sleeve and grunted, "It sure is hot outside! Hoeing out those ole' thistles was an awful job, an' my hands are full of stickers."

"You oughta' be glad you have hands to work with," I said trying to practice gladness. "Some people don't even have hands. I read once about a girl who was born without any."

The look Wilbur shot my way was not exactly one of appreciation or approval.

—"When are we gonna' eat dinner? I'm gettin' hungry," Frances whined.

"You oughta' be glad you have food to eat and that you're not one of the 'starving Armenians.' "

—"Ruth, you and Mary get the fly bushes and chase the flies outa' the dining room before supper," instructed Mother.

"Why do I have to do that all the time? Why can't Esther or Frances do it sometimes? They always get off easier than the rest of us," Mary complained.

"You can be glad you have flies to . . . uh . . . , that you don't have to chase flies in the winter time."

—"Why do we always have to pick up the apples for schnitzing?" asked Frances. "Why can't Bertha or Ruth or Mary do that sometimes? I don't care if they are bigger."

"I don't like to pick up apples either, but I guess I'm glad we have apples."

—"I wish it wasn't so hot! I'm burnin' up. Do you think it'll ever cool off?"

"You oughta' be glad it isn't freezin' like it was last winter. It's better now than it was then."

—One evening after milking was over Jake came in stewing, "The flies were awful on the cows this evening. Old Black Cow kept tryin' to get 'em off and she switched and switched me across the face. I got so mad I'd like to take a switch to her."

"Did she have any manure on her tail like they do sometimes? If she didn't you can sure be glad for that."

—"Esther didn't wash her feet, why do I have to wash mine?" Frances growled.

"Cause yours are dirty and mine aren't, that's why. As dirty as you are, you oughta' be glad Mother didn't make you wash all over."

—One day at the dinner table I fumed, "Yesterday evening while we were at Yager's Store I saw Tommy Crow and he called me 'Dumb Dutchman' again. He said, 'What are you doin' Dumb Dutchman?' He makes me so mad!"

"What's wrong, Esther, can't you find somethin' to be glad about?"

"Yeh, Esther, you oughta' be glad he didn't call you the dumbest Dutchman."

"Let's stop the foolish talk now," Pappy ordered, interrupting the bickering. "All of you ought to be glad for your Dutch heritage (he didn't yet know about the 'glad game'). Your ancestors were God fearing people who left Germany many years ago and came to America to find a place where they could worship as they pleased. They came to Pennsylvania and later some of them left there and moved down into this beautiful Shenandoah Valley. They built their homes here and tilled the fertile land. Neighbor helped neighbor in time of need. They built their churches where they came together on Sundays for worship and fellowship. They were a good and honest people; it has often been said of the Brethren, 'their word is as good as their bond.' "

By now I felt a bit ashamed of my outburst, so I rather meekly said, "Yes, Pappy, since you told us that, I'm glad I am Dutch and I won't pay any attention to Tommy Crow next time he calls me Dumb Dutchman. But I hope he doesn't do it again."

—"Children, it's about time you go to bed; we have lots to do tomorrow so you need your rest," Mother suggested.

"Aw why do we have to go to bed this soon?" Wilbur grumbled. "I'm not through with my book yet."

"You oughta' be glad you have a bed to sleep in. I hear some people have to sleep on the floor."

"What's all this stuff about being glad all the time?" asked Wilbur who was by now becoming a little irritated at my excesses.

"That's the game Pollyanna played; she called it the 'glad game,' " I answered. "It's a nice game."

"Pollyanna! Who's Pollyanna?" he queried again.

" 'Pollyanna' and 'Pollyanna Grows Up' are novels. If you'd read something besides history all the time you'd know who she was! Why don't you read some good books?"

Wilbur shot back, "Who wants to read all those silly love stories? You're the one who oughta' be readin' books that are worth somethin'."

Weddings: Orthodox and Otherwise

Cherry picking, seeding, and canning time was finally over; I was glad for that. Only yesterday, the day seemed to be forever, we had gone over to the "Gravels" where Pappy bought a tree of sour cherries. We picked the fruit from the ground, standing on ladders, or climbing the tree. We each had a gallon bucket or milk bucket with a hand-fashioned wire hook that held the container on the limb. When we had filled a bucket we emptied it into a washtub. By the time we had stripped the tree bare we had just about a tub full. All morning and into the afternoon we had been washing and seeding and canning. Now that everything was about finished, Frances and I slipped off to the front yard to swing on the new rope swing that Jasper had just recently fastened to a large limb in one of the maple trees. By the time we had made it to the front yard a buggy drove up to the gate and stopped. In it sat a young man and a girl. The man called to us, "Girls, is your Pappy at home? We come to git married and we want him to tie the knot for us."

"He's around here somewhere. We'll go and ask Mother where he is," was our answer, and we scurried across the yard to the back porch.

"Mother, where's Pappy? A couple just drove up to the front gate in a buggy and said they wanted to get married and they wanted Pappy to tie the knot; that's what they said," I reported all out of breath from running and talking in one continuous stream.

"Oh my, he and the boys are out in the field thinning corn. Mary, you run out there and get him right away; you can find him quicker than Esther and Frances can," Mother instructed.

She pulled off her soiled apron, washed her hands, and brushed her hair back from her face to go to the front to invite the couple in. Elizabeth, Bertha and Ruth also tidied up a bit and we all followed Mother to the front yard. The couple had a built-in congregation, a crowd of witnesses, whether they wanted it or not. We were to soon learn that they probably would have preferred not to have an audience.

"It is pretty hot out here, won't you get out and come in the house?" Mother invited.

"We're in a hurry, so we'll just stay in the buggy. T'won't be long 'til he gits here will it?" was their question of concern, and for some reason they both giggled.

It wasn't long before Pappy appeared, still in his work clothes and with his Bible in his hand.

After a minimum of formality he said, "I'm ready now, so if you'll just get out of the buggy and give me your license we'll go into the yard under the tree and perform the ceremony."

"We don't wanna' git out. Can't we just set here in the buggy and you perform the weddin' thata' way?" they asked. "We're in a hurry."

"No, I don't believe we can do that. I think it is customary for couples to stand together in front of the minister when the vows are taken."

The man, hunching the girl with his elbow, said, "G'wan, git out; looks like we're gonna' hafta'."

Finally, after the persuasion by Pappy, they slowly and somewhat clumsily clambered down out of the buggy, particularly the bride. But they refused to come any further and insisted on standing between the wheels of the vehicle. Immediately it was quite obvious why she was reluctant to comply. We didn't know whether she was too late married or too soon pregnant. As folks expressed it in those days, she was very much in a "family way," out of wedlock. It's questionable whether any minister ever performed a wedding before with the bride and groom flanked by two buggy wheels, but Pappy, without further insistence, proceeded with the ceremony:

> God saw from the beginning that it was not good for man to be alone, so he made for him a helpmeet in the person of a woman. She was not to be taken from his head to be lorded over by him, nor from his feet to be trampled under foot, but from his side nearest his heart to be cherished, loved, and protected.
>
> Will you now join your right hands? Do you . . . . take this woman to be your lawful wedded wife, to love, cherish, and protect her until death do you part?
>
> If so, say I do.
>
> 'I do.'
>
> Do you . . . . take this man to be your lawful wedded husband, to love, cherish, and protect him until death do you part?

If so, say I do.

'I do.'

I now pronounce you man and wife.

What God hath joined together let not man put asunder.

Let us pray:

Our kind Father in heaven, we ask Thy blessing upon this man and this woman. Guide them and care for them. May they love each other as God loves them. We pray that Thou wilt always be a welcome guest in their home and that they will bring up their children in the fear and admonition of the Lord.

Bless this union and may they always be true to each other and to Thee and at last enter Thy blessed Kingdom.

Through Christ our Lord. Amen.

Our ways of having fun were many and varied, usually not meant to be disrespectful or thoughtless. Perhaps sometimes a bit irreverant and colorful when our imaginations were on the loose, and irrepressible, as was true when we held mock weddings, quite often after Pappy performed cermonies.

We followed his pattern rather carefully with someone personifying the bride, the groom and the minister (often played by Bertha who knew every word of Pappy's ceremony from beginning to end) and the remaining participants became witnesses. The ceremony was duly recited, the vows were taken and the prayer was prayed. Then came the final statement, and we suddenly deviated from the orthodox and pronounced:

What God hath joined asunder
Let not man separate together.

Days of the week were designated by the chores performed, almost as frequently as by their given names. Monday—lines of clothes flying in the breeze—wash day. Tuesday—black flat irons heating on the stove and a basket of dampened down clothes—ironing day. Saturday—ten, twelve pies waiting their turns for baking in the big black oven—baking day. And in between—cleaning days.

One Monday, Frances and I had just finished scouring up the front porch with the left over wash water, when we saw and heard Uncle Charlie's little runabout chugging down the road, then stopping at the front gate. We dashed into the front room, the screen door banging behind us.

"Mother! Mother!" we called. "Uncle Charlie just stopped at the front gate!"

The answer came back, "Invite him in, girls, while I take off my apron and wash my hands."

"Come on in," I said, trying to be polite as Mother had instructed. "Have a chair; Mother will be here in a minute. We are glad to see you." ("glad game" again).

"Thank you, girls." Then he proceeded to ask the inevitable question that he had been asking us ever since we had done a cut-up job on our clothes some years before, which began by our snipping the sleeves from our dresses, then taking off our brown cotton cloth drawers and cutting both in quite unsquared squares. In the end becoming frightened at our own questionable act, we had packed them in Mother's and Pappy's potty and pushed them far back under their bed.

"Girls have you been cutting any quilt squares lately?" he chided and threw back his head with good-humored laughter. Uncle Charlie enjoyed his sister Mary's big family immensely, but none of our escapades more than this one.

By now Mother had tidied herself and had joined us in the front room.

"Good morning, Brother Charlie."

"Good morning, Sister Mary. I just spent the morning over at the Bowmans and I thought you'd like to know that they have a new baby girl."

"Well, well, another girl," Mother mused. "Do they have a name for her yet, or have they run out of girl names?"

"They have named her Rachel; she is a nice baby and everyone seems to be doing fine."

"That's good. I'm always glad to hear that."

Then Uncle Charlie turned to another subject. "I guess you have noticed by the papers that there is right much infantile paralysis over the country this summer, and recently there are some cases around in Rockingham County. Since we doctors don't know exactly how it gets spread, maybe the children shouldn't be going to places where lots of people, especially children, are gathered. Other than that, you'll just have to take care of yourselves as best you can."

In those days there were several dreaded childhood diseases, among them whooping cough, diptheria, measles and infantile paralysis which so often was fatal, or at other times left children terribly crippled. We had no antitoxins or antibiotics to prevent these epidemics, we could only suffer through them and hopefully make it.

At that moment, Mother noticed Frances trying to peer through the round stovepipe hole in the firescreen covering the fireplace. "Frances, you'd better get away from there before you get into trouble," she warned, thinking back to an incident of a few years past.

"It sounds like birds chirping in the 'chimley'," Frances explained. "And I just wanted to see them."

"Yes, I think some chimney sweeps have their nest there in the chimney. They've been making a lotta' noise lately. But I don't want the same thing happenin' to you that happened to Mary when she was small." Then turning to Uncle Charlie she told the story of what had happened to Mary.

"When Wilbur was a baby Aunt Patty Mac was here helping for awhile. One day Mary, for some reason, stuck her head in that hole there in the fireplace screen and she couldn't get it out. She screamed and yelled until Aunt Patty who finally heard her came running and saw her problem. Aunt Patty turned, and jiggled, and screwed Mary's head around until at last she got it out, to Mary's great relief. Mary's face and head were just covered with black soot and all streaked with her tears."

Now Uncle Charlie had another funny story to enjoy, which he did at that moment with another hearty laugh.

His car had just disappeared in its cloud of dust down the road when we heard the chug-chug of another motor going by the house and then suddenly stopping. The sound of a car engine was still rare enough to always catch our attention. By the time Mother, Frances and I had returned to the kitchen, the driver of this vehicle appeared at the back porch carrying a dead chicken.

"Mrs. Pence, I'm very sorry but I hit one of your chickens with my car. I didn't see it crossin' the road. It doesn't seem like it's bruised up much. I thought maybe you could still use it. I'll be glad to pay you whatever it's worth."

"No indeed, we wouldn't let you pay anything for it, and we thank you for bringing it in. Its body is still warm and it doesn't seem to be torn up much so I believe we can use it."

In those times chickens were not constantly housed but were allowed the freedom to roam about, and as to be expected they sometimes wandered to the road. And even with the limited number of cars, one would occasionally get hit. Usually when this happened the driver of the vehicle would stop and take the chicken to the house, if it were not too badly mangled to be salvaged; often times he offered to pay for it. We always hoped it would not be a laying hen, but cars were no respectors of chickens. It so happened that this one was salvageable, so Ruth proceeded to chop off its head, scald it in boiling water, and pluck its feathers. It was then dressed and salted down in a crock. At least we could look forward to a good chicken potpie for dinner on Tuesday.

Grapes and Comfortable Piety

Dog Days again had passed, and we were on the way to the Big Rock to go swimming while the weather was still warm. We threaded our way through the thistles and nettles in the meadow until we reached the swimming hole. We were never bothered by having to change clothes, as our dresses were our swim suits, but to our disappointment the water was low and scummy since there had been no recent rains. The snake doctors and skippers flew around us incessantly, skimming over the water.

"This is no fun!" Mary complained.

"This is a mess!"

"Let's get out and take a walk down along the river. I bet we could see the rocks clear across the river the water is so low."

We clambered up the bank at that suggestion, still finding it necessary to pull the leaches off our legs, even though we had been in the water only a few minutes.

It was still early in the afternoon so we felt no urge to hurry. We loitered along the bank of the river, stopping occasionally to glance across its expanse.

"Hey, I saw a fish jump out of the water!"

"I bet I could wade out to the rocks, the river is so low."

"Don't you dare to try it! There are lots of deep holes that fool you sometimes. When you step off one of those rock ledges you go way down."

"Look at those big ole' trees with the white limbs. Did somebody whitewash them?" Virginia asked.

"No, you silly goose! They're sycamore trees!"

"They look like skeletons to me."

"I think they kinda' look like ghosts. They're scary lookin'."

"You can be glad they're not real ghosts." (My Pollyanna comment).

"The grasshoppers sure are thick around here, they keep bumpin' my face and legs."

"Not many flowers bloomin' anymore, just a lot of dry grass and a few fall asters."

"Ouch! I stepped on some stickers! Wait 'til I pick this one out of my foot."

By now a ramshackle frame house sitting back some yards from the river caught our attention.

"Look at that ole' broken down house!"

"Looks like it's about ready to fall to pieces!"

"It kinda' 'skeers' me. I wonder if it's haunted."

"There's no such thing as haunts."

And there upon ensued our usual arguments about the authenticity of ghosts and haunts.

"There is, too, ghosts and haunts. My mother said so!"

"Well our Pappy says that's nuthin' but a supersitition."

"One of our neighbors said they heard them makin' awful noises when they went past the ole' Brown house."

"It probably was nuthin' but the wind or an ole' screech owl or somethin'."

Suddenly Frances D. interrupted the argument with a shout, "Hey, look at all those grapes on that vine there!"

Sure enough, what was left of the front porch was giving way to the weight of a rambling grapevine that was crawling across the roof and twining around each of the gray weather beaten posts slanting obliquely at a treacherous angle. It covered the ground where the porch had been, its errant branches contorting their way through the paneless windows. It was laden with bunches of deep purple grapes that seemed to be the sole feast of the bees and fall insects.

"Oh boy, let's get some of them to eat! They are just goin' to waste."

"Yeh, let's do; they sure look good!"

"I'm hungry, and thirsty, too."

"But that would be stealin' wouldn't it?"

"I guess it would be and the Bible says stealin' is a sin."

"What can we do? I sure would like to have some."

"Me too."

"Me too."

We weren't stymied for long. As usual Frances D. had a brainstorm, "I'll tell ya' what, Virginia, you haven't joined the church yet, so it won't make any difference if you do it. The rest of us have already joined except you and Ruth, so it would be wrong for us to take them."

"Yeh, I can't do it, 'cause I belong to the church."

"Me too, I joined last year."

We were all too eager to acquiese to Frances' questionable plan.

"I was just baptized," right on down until Virginia and Ruth were the only two unchurched ones.

"That's a good idea. Virginia, it won't be so bad for you to do it. You can pull off the bunches and Ruth can carry them to the rest of us."

And Margaret and Elizabeth promised, "We won't tell Mother on you."

After this unorthodox rationalizing and pressure from us, Virginia and Ruth reluctantly approached the vine and Virginia began pulling off the bunches and handing them to Ruth who in turn brought them to us.

We put them on a pile and sat in an irregular circle surrounding this potential feast, waiting until we had a sufficiency and Virginia and Ruth could join us, trying to be magnanimous after the questionable way we had used them.

As they squeezed into the circle, "You can be glad you don't belong to the church, 'cause if you were a member God would probably get you for what you did." (My next Pollyanna remark).

Grapes were never sweeter or more delicious! We sucked the juice and grapes from the hulls letting them slip down our throats with gusto and satisfaction. We relaxed lazily as we spat the hulls on the ground around us—satisfied that we had kept our heavenly records untarnished.

Country Ham: Good! and Kosher??

When sowing and harvesting and preserving times have ended, farm folks begin to make preparations for what lies ahead: school, cold weather, short days, and long nights. This time had come again, thus Mother was busy at the sewing machine making gingham school dresses for Frances and me. Elizabeth was helping with the designing (with patterns cut from newspaper) as she seemed to have some expertise in fashions. I loved the colorful blue gingham and the way it was turning into a pretty dress.

Looking up from her sewing, Mother said to me, "Esther, run into my bedroom and get the liniment bottle off my bureau. My shears are getting real dull. I want to sharpen them a little."

Anxious to help the project along I complied, and brought the bottle to her immediately. Mother opened the scissors on the neck of the bottle and as she sharpened them it appeared as though she were trying to cut the bottle neck.

When Frances and I were small Mother usually dressed us like twins. There were no hand-me-downs to Frances from me. What I had in height she made up for in breadth, so she could never wear a dress that I had outgrown. Besides, when a dress became a little short and our arms extended too far beyond the sleeves, they were simply turned into everyday dresses and eventually worn out.

I am sure there were times when Mother and Pappy wondered how they would dress and coat and shoe eleven growing children, but this year both Bertha and Elizabeth would be teaching and Charlie was on his own. A favorable season had produced a rather bountiful wheat and corn crop, and Mother's flock of turkeys had matured without great loss and were almost ready for marketing. I was *glad, glad, glad* when Mother decided that Frances and I should each have a new coat for the winter, since our old ones were both shabby and small.

Wednesday morning came. Frances and I bustled about getting ready for the trip to town, but Mother and Pappy didn't seem to bustle much. They sat relaxed and unhurried at the breakfast table listening to the early morning family chatter. At intervals they poured the coffee from their cups into the saucers to cool it, and sipped it leisurely, enjoying the last drop.

Frances and I continued to fidget, until Mother finally suggested, "Esther, I think you and Frances could go wash your faces and hands now and start getting ready."

We waited for no further instructions but dashed out to the kitchen and the family wash pan.

"They'd better hurry up and get dressed or we'll be late," I confided to Frances.

"Yeh, I'm afraid so, too." Frances agreed.

Just what we would be late to was never quite certain.

We tripped up the stairs and pulled on our good dresses posthaste. Ruth, who needed some material to make a few things before she went back to the Academy, soon joined us.

Mother was making some ham sandwiches to take along for dinner. Jasper had backed the car from the car shed and was checking the gas. This was accomplished by taking up the front seat under which the tank was located, then inserting a measuring stick in it to determine the amount of gas it contained. Soon we were on our way. Trips to Harrisonburg were rare enough that the scenery in the countryside was still new and mindboggling to Frances and me, so we were constantly posing questions:

"Who lives in that pretty brick house?"

"What kinda' car was that we just met?"

"What'll they do with all those apples the men are pickin'? Those sure are big orchards!"

"My goodness! Look at all those cows! Who do you reckon milks all of them? I'm sure glad I don't hafta'."

"Look at all those gooses over there in that pond! Aren't they pretty?"

"They're not gooses, Frances, they're geese."

"What's that awful roarin' noise over our heads?"

"It's an airplane!" shouted Ruth, sticking her head out of the car and looking up to spot it.

Jasper slowed the car enough so that we could all catch a glimpse of one of the early biplanes which on rare occasions passed over the Valley.

And the inevitable and oft repeated question, "How long will it be 'til we get there?"

Our destination was B. Ney's Store, where we bought most of our clothes that couldn't be stitched together on our sewing machine.

Our first mission was to make Ruth's purchases in the dry goods department, then all four of us walked up the broad squeaky wooden steps to the second floor.

By the time we had reached this landing, Mr. Carl Ney of Ladies and Children's Ready-to-Wear greeted us with the "Good Morning" of a practiced salesman.

"What can I help you with today, Mrs. Pence?"

Mother set her basket down on a nearby table and replied. "Esther and Frances need coats, we'd like to look at what you have."

"Well you came to the right place; we just got in a shipment of children's coats. Just look through this rack and see if you can find something you like. There are some real fine bargains and we'll make you a real good price."

"I think this red one is real pretty," I observed, hopefully.

"I'm afraid that one would show dirt mighty quickly."

"How do you girls like these deep blue ones?" asked Ruth who was trying to help us make our choices.

"I think they are real pretty; the velvet collars feel so nice and soft."

Mother after checking the price tag, said to Mr. Ney, "The price is far too high. I can't afford to pay that much."

"But that is such a fine piece of cloth, Mrs. Pence, just feel that quality," said Mr. Ney, inviting Mother to handle it. "Let's try them on, girls, and see it they fit."

We were glad to oblige and were soon preening ourselves in front of the thin mirror.

"Yes, they are nice coats and they look real good on the girls, but I just can't afford to put out eighteen dollars for two coats," was Mother's assessment, shattering our hopes to little bits.

"They are just eight ninety eight a piece, Mrs. Pence, the two would come to only seventeen ninety six. I'll tell you what, since you are buying two, how does sixteen ninety eight sound to you?"

"Still too much, Mr. Ney," Mother said as she started to hang the coats back on the rack to our great dismay.

Mr. Ney scratched his head as he did some figuring on a pad in his well-cultivated whisper that he used on all his customers, "For you, Mrs. Pence, I'll let the two coats go for sixteen dollars. That has to be my last offer."

So he thought.

At that moment he caught the smell of Mother's country ham sandwiches on the table nearby, "Mrs. Pence, do I smell ham sandwiches on some of your homemade bread in that basket?"

"Yes, I packed some for our dinner today," Mother replied.

At that point his appetite for country ham and homemade bread overpowered his obedience to his Hebraic traditions and ham became Kosher.

"Mrs. Pence, would you sell me a couple of those sandwiches? I know I'm not supposed to eat ham, but they smell so good I feel like I just have to have some."

Mother studied a minute and then said, "I'll let you have them if you'll sell me those two coats for fifteen dollars. But I don't take any responsibility for your breaking your religious rules."

"Mrs. Pence, you are a hard bargainer. I know we Jews are noted for that, but you would qualify to be one of us any day. I guess I'll have to say that you've made a deal."

Beneath Mother's soft serene exterior and her unruffled mien there was a practicality and intelligence that sometimes surprised even those who knew her well. But little did she know, at this moment, that the profit on this sale might, in a small way, benefit the recipients of Mr. Ney's generosity, sometimes the very poor to whom he would furnish items of clothing. He was recognized for his philanthropy, and among his beneficiaries was the Mack Memorial Library at Bridgewater College.

Mr. Ney got his ham sandwiches and, to Frances' and my delight, we got our coats.

As we made our departure, Mr. Ney carried his part of the bargain into a small room at the back of the store to avoid interruptions from customers, and for one meal his diet was the best that farmers thereabouts could offer.

Bushes and Burns

When frosts came we knew that winter was not far behind, but we clung to outdoor activities as long as the balmy Indian Summer days remained. The coming of frost wrought many changes to the countryside, among them was the splitting open of the chinquapin burrs and the spilling of the nuts that had been held captive in their prickly bearded prisons. We had often handled burrs and prickly things before, but none so painful to the fingers as "chinkapins." Yet we tended to forget or ignore that fact when we remembered how good they were after we, like squirrels, would bite open each little nut and find the kernel within. They did not fall at our feet like manna from heaven and they didn't jump out at us when we went chinquapinning.

Frances D., Margaret, Elizabeth, Mary, Frances and I planned our excursion to the "Flat Woods" beyond Port Republic at the foot of the mountain, where the chinquapins grew.

On Saturday morning, a convoy of two buggies was on its way quite a distance from home, without too much prospect of success. Somehow that didn't concern us greatly. When we arrived at what appeared to be a promising area, we hopped down and tied our horses to trees. All around us were low scrubby bushes of various shapes, sizes and varieties, including chinquapins. Each of us had a cloth sugar poke, optimistically hoping to fill it. If there is a skill in gleaning chinquapins, we didn't have it. The barbs were so prickly and hostile to the fingers that it was almost a question of who was attacking whom. We almost gave up in despair. Finally we began looking for burrs already popped open and still holding a nut; at least we didn't have to split them. Of course, this limited the number we were able to gather. Fortunately there was no reason to be in a big hurry, except for the distance of the return trip. The sun was still rather high in the sky, so we wandered here and there over the field that appeared to be not anyone's land in particular. We each roamed over our own chosen path until by and by Mary suddenly missed our Frances.

"Hey! Do any of you see Frances anywhere?" she asked with concern.

We all raised up from our stoop positions and began gazing around us.

"I don't see her anywhere!"

"Neither do I; I wonder where she could be."

"I'll look over this way. Fran—ces! Fran—ces! Fran—ces!"

"And I'll look in this direction. Frances! Fran—ces! Fran—ces! Frances, can you hear me? Where are you?"

We ran hither and thither, calling anxiously over and over, "Fran—ces! Fran—ces! Where are you?"

At last Margaret called excitedly, "Here she is! I found her!"

We all ran in the direction of Margaret's voice to where Frances had disappeared over a rise in the ground and was sitting down by a little stream.

"Frances! What are you doin' down there? You oughta' know better'n goin' away from the rest of us like that! You scared us half to death!" exclaimed Mary, almost too relieved to scold very severely.

"I was just lookin' at the minnows. See all those little fishes swimmin' around in there? I lost my sugar poke and started lookin' for it, but I couldn't find it anywhere, and then I saw this 'crick' with all the little fishes in it. I was watchin' them."

"Well you oughta' know better'n wanderin' off like that, you could'a got lost! What if we hadn't found you?" Mary finally found her feisty tongue.

"Where are your 'chinkapins'?" I asked.

"I told ya', I lost my poke!" Frances replied, becoming a little feisty herself.

"I bet if she picked any she ate 'em all, as usual," I said accusingly.

"Esther, you oughta' at least be glad we found her," countered Frances D.

I looked at her quizzically, not quite knowing how to take that statement, but wondering if she were taunting me with my "glad game."

"Well, before anything else happens I think we'd better be gettin' home," Mary suggested.

We all agreed. With sore pricked fingers and very few chinquapins, we climbed into our buggies.

With a little click in the back of their throats and a cracking of the reins in their hands, Mary and Frances D. headed their horses homeward.

"Hey, did you bring us some 'chinkapins'?" Wilbur inquired the instant we stepped into the house.

Mary and I each had a few handfuls in the bottoms of our pokes to show for our afternoon's labor.

"Gee whiz! Is that all you got for bein' gone a whole afternoon?" Jake asked, scornfully looking at our cache.

"Well you just go and try to pick those sticky scratchy things yourself, if you think it's so easy!" I answered crossly.

Mary decided it best not to tell that Frances got away from us for a while, at least she didn't mention it. But she did justify our small hoard by saying, "I'll tell you one thing, they are the hardest things to get out of those burrs I ever saw. My fingers are so sore I don't think I can do my milkin' this evening."

"Me neither," I quickly agreed.

"Huh! You're sure not gonna' get outa' milkin' that easy! I'm not gonna' do it for you!" Wilbur shot back.

"Me neither," was Jake's fast rejoinder.

"Esther, you oughta' be glad you didn't have to pick 'chinkapins' with your nose. How would you like to have *it* all stuck up?" Wilbur nettled me.

That was the second time this afternoon the "glad game" had lampooned me.

Finally Pappy broke up the combativeness by reminding us:

> Nothing is gotten without hard work.
> No rose without its thorns.
> No chinquapins without its burrs.

There was something about going to school in the fall that cleansed the spirit of summer excesses and petty quarrels, the hangovers from the season's doldrums and the monotony of daily farm chores. Perhaps it was the brisk walk to school on a crisp fall morning; perhaps it was the challenge of a higher grade with its addition of fresh subjects to learn; perhaps new fascinating stories in a more advanced reader; perhaps going to the blackboard and diagramming sentences with some confidence and skill; perhaps outdistancing a schoolmate in a race on the playground at recess time. There were many perhaps for me as I entered school each new term, for school was never an affliction but a challenge and a satisfaction. Pappy and Mother had somehow inspired most of their children in a quest for knowledge and impressed upon them the importance of an education.

I suppose what really happened was that school hastened the demise of the "glad game," which was already beginning to grow stale and wearisome. I indulged in anger and irritation like most normal youngsters, and I didn't always want to say, "I'm sorry" or "I'm glad" this or that didn't happen. My indulgences and excesses in trying to be Pollyanna were not endearing me to my brothers and sisters and playmates. I certainly was not making any new friends nor influencing people.

I hadn't found any cross old ladies or grouchy old men in my neighborhood to whom I could be "Little Miss Sunshine," or any sick folks to whom I could be an angel of mercy like Pollyanna, so that dream fell through the cracks to reality also. And for sure, I hadn't learned to know, as Pollyanna did, any orphan boy or any rich man who became his adopted father, so how could I some day marry an orphan who became the son of a rich man?

Rich man, poor man,
Beggar man, thief,
Doctor, lawyer,
Indian chief.

Housewife, teacher,

. . . . . .
Nurse, . . .

"glad
girl"

Again, I had lost a button.

PART FOUR: THE YEAR OF "ME"

The day before yesterday Pappy came in from the outdoors and made a gloomy weather forecast, "I just saw a 'sun dog' in the sky. That's a sign it will probably rain soon."

"Aw no, I hope not!"

"Don't let it rain!"

"Rain would spoil everything!"

But rain it did. Yesterday it began, but preparations for the wedding went on; the house was cleaned; the cakes were baked: Elizabeth's coconut cake, Mary's devil's food cake, Mother's pound cake, Bertha's checkerboard cake, and Ruth's wedding cake—the second one after the first one went flat.

Then Ruth's wedding day dawned—still rainy and dreary, but by and by the showers fell intermittently, finally stopped altogether. Then there appeared in the sky a "patch of blue big enough to make a pair of overalls," and we felt assured it was going to clear up. We were not disappointed.

I went to the fields to gather daisies for the arch in the yard and we entwined them with the honeysuckle. The weather was finally in league with us. The wedding took place at the appointed hour, as the sun was setting in a washed and luminous sky. Friends and relatives fellowshipped; the cakes all disappeared; the bride and groom disappeared, too, vanished before any bellers or pranksters were aware. Many "just marrieds" were not as elusive as Ruth and her new husband. And if they weren't so lucky the neighborhood yokels might pull a prank or bell them. More often the bellers would appear on the return from the honeymoon and perform a nuptial serenade. These rustic serenaders gathered, usually past bedtime, with their assorted noise makers: cowbells, kettles, pots and pans of all varities and conditions, sometimes a circular saw, the most dissonant instrument of all. Suddenly with a one-a, two-a, three-a, the awful din began. Their objective was to induce the new bride and groom to appear, and the clamor usually continued until the response came. After a few applications of unpolished country humor to embarrass them, they expected the couple to kiss, and if they cooperated in this, then the group would disband and be gone.

Tonight we were spared the trauma, and as I helped Elizabeth carry the wedding presents upstairs, I remarked, "Well the wedding is over and it went off real good. These sure are nice gifts."

On the next morning as I went about my usual chores I remembered something I had come upon the day before while I was picking daisies from a clump at the edge of the cornfield. A beautiful pale green chrysalis with tiny dots of gold was hanging by a thin frail thread from a blade of corn. I had carefully broken off the blade, carried it with me to the house and placed it in a rosebush in the front yard. As soon as my work was finished I hurried to inspect the state of the chrysalis. It was still there, but a change was taking place from the forces of the life within. The beautiful green color had become dull and nondescript. The covering of the chrysalis seemed to be tightly inflated. As I watched, the jacket began to split open and new life emerged, the long body of a butterfly with its wings folded so tightly against its torso so that their color was barely visible. I held out my finger and the caterpillar like creature crawled onto it and clung quietly there. Then began the development of its wings that was beautiful and fascinating to behold. As they fanned gently and silently back and forth, the drying and unfolding took place, until there was a full-blown monarch butterfly. I stood quietly watching with awe, almost afraid to move lest I scare this beautiful and gentle creature. Finally flexing its wings in one great sweep it took flight. I watched it soar into the distance until it disappeared and my eyes could no longer follow.

There comes a time when families, too, break the bonds that bind them together—the children develop and grow, try their wings, and take flight.

The separation is felt more poignantly by the remnant that is left at home when this process begins and the ties are broken.

Ruth was now making preparations to establish a home of her own.

Elizabeth would soon be returning to the classroom, the work she loved dearly and in which she was so successful.

Charlie was now rather premanently settled in a job in the city, working in a Piggly Wiggly grocery store.

And then for the first time, Wilbur and Mary would be tugging at the family ties. They were preparing to go to Weyers Cave to complete their last two years of high school and would return home only for the weekends. In those days there were very few local high schools and no yellow buses to haul us to the distant ones.

Jake, Frances, and I would remain on the farm. Fortunately for this younger trio, and also for Mother and Pappy and Jasper, Bertha was now teaching at Timber Ridge and living at home, which would soften the pangs of separation.

We were moving rapidly into this another autumn in the life of our family, with adjustments having to be made to these changes and separations. The beginning of one more year of school was only a short distance behind. The signs were telling us this was so. The coats of the farm animals, which had been sparse and ragged through the hot summer months, were growing thick and glossy in preparation for the cold months ahead. Chickens, too, that had shed their feathers and had been partly naked in the summer heat were now feathering out again with full shiny coats. That is, all except one—one old hen that seemed to defy all the laws of nature and common sense continued to run around the farm in the nude. That seemed appropriate as long as the weather remained warm, but now that fall days were descending and a chill was in the air such behavior didn't seem timely or natural. What quirk of nature took place that prevented the growth of her feathers we never knew, but we could observe that here was a creature not at all prepared for the impending low temperatures.

One day after this state of affairs had continued for a time and Mother's sympathy for this poor helpless one increased, she came up with a solution, "I hate to see the poor old thing standing around shivering in such misery like that. I think I'll try to make an outfit for her. Maybe her feathers will finally grow out, and in the meantime that might help to keep her warm."

Having said this she proceeded to carry out her good intentions. She took one of Pappy's heavy but well worn cotton socks and cut off the foot part. She drew one end together with thread, leaving just enough room to allow the hen's head to go through. She cut holes to make room for the feet to get out, and then made little legs from the extra sock material to fit the hen's shanks and sewed them in place. Now to catch the victim. This wasn't difficult since she was too chilled to be very active at this point. Mother slipped this unique outfit over her head, pulled it back over the naked body, poking the legs through in the process. I dare say that no other hen before or since had been seen in such regalia. Thereafter she was a comical bird, strutting around the farm like a member of her opposite sex, quite content in this new apparel. Her appreciation was apparent; before too long she became a real friend, permitting us to pet her at any time, often sidling up to us as if to say, "Thank you." We were sure she would have been perfectly content to live in the house with the family without any fear. But how do you housebreak a chicken? When the weather turned bleak and even colder, we noticed that her tail feathers were sprouting and her whole outfit appeared to be burgeoning with feathers, perhaps nurtured by the warmth of her garb. Finally, Mother cut off the sock suit. There our pet stood, well covered with a soft glossy coat, but still cuddling against Mother, trying to express her gratitude.

With the disappearing of hot weather and the reappearing of a well-feathered flock, our egg production increased. As farmers, we were grateful for this, since it always meant more eggs to trade for necessary and useful items.

On a farm, time slips naturally and tranquilly into fall, the passing of a milestone that often goes unnoticed. This was so in the life span of our family, and even though there were internal changes as the children grew and matured, the customs and routines of our farm life changed slowly. With the coming of fall, the same preparations to the cold months ahead took place as usual. Pappy and Jasper went to the woods with the big farm wagon and cross-cut saw to fell trees and haul them in, readying them for sawing and chopping into stove-sized pieces. Our woodpile grew bigger and bigger. Mother made a new batch of homemade soap and stored it in the wash house. The apple butter had been boiled, crocked and stored for use in school dinner pails. Sauerkraut was already fermenting and smelling in a ten gallon stone jar in the cellar. Dried beans had been harvested, shelled, and winnowed for a family who loved beans. A large heap of potatoes lay in their bin in the dark cool cellar. Pappy and the boys had picked the plump rosy apples, some were stored in the cellar for daily use, others covered with corn fodder in the barn to prevent freezing, and the rest buried in the garden for protection. We had a poke of dried apple schnitz for stewing and for schnitz and dumplings. After threshing, we had filled our bed ticks with fresh straw for warmer and more comfortable sleeping through the winter, since the old straw had been 'rootshed' down and so thoroughly pulverized that we could feel the bed ropes or slats through our ticks. The flour chest in the pantry was filled almost to capacity for a good winter's supply. Our wardrobes had been replenished only when something had worn out or we had outgrown some garment. Jasper half-soled shoes where the uppers appeared to have enough wear in them to justify this. Most families owned a shoe-last and kept a supply of tacks for this purpose. Mother patched and darned long underwear and sewed on buttons where replacements were needed, and they were ready for occupancy. Bed covers were taken out of storage to be available for the cold nights that were sure to come.

Jake had the rabbit trap business all to himself this winter, since Wilbur was away at school. He was now setting his traps in all the usual grazing spots, hoping to ensnare those that frequented our field and meadows.

Each day we traversed the familiar road to school, dinner pails swinging and blue denim book satchels riding our shoulders. The book satchels held our dog-eared, finger-smudged books, a new Big Top tablet thick and rough, a new pencil with unused, unchewed eraser, and a supply of apples tucked here and there in the corners.

Along the woods the ground squirrels were scurrying hither and thither, looking for some last tidbits of food before they closed their tunnel doors to sleep through the long winter.

By the corn shocks lay piles of golden corn that Pappy and Jasper had been shucking each day to be soon hauled to the corn crib before the first snow fell. The crows raucously calling to each other were zeroing in on the piles, sneaking their breakfast before Pappy and Jasper came to the field and scared them away.

Up the hills and down we shuffled along with our friends; any new pairs of shoes would soon take on the weathered look of age and stress. Reviewing their appearance when butchering time came, we would likely grease them with tallow to extend their life. This school year was a milestone in my life, one that did not pass by unnoticed, as I enrolled in high school for the first time. I sensed my new growing up status. At least I was no longer foolish enough to pull some of the silly tricks of the past year, such as the time Elizabeth and I rubbed coal on our faces to attract attention when the teacher had sent us to the coal house to bring in a scuttle full. It was stimulating to discover a new kind of mathematics, algebra with its equations and searchings for the unknown; to read some of the great classics, "Silas Marner," "David Copperfield," "The Call of the Wild."

Our days and hours were busy ones. Each evening as soon as school was out, we walked briskly down the road to our home. Jake immediately changed from his school clothes into his everyday ones and went to the field to help Jasper shuck corn. That left the evening's milking for Frances and me, along with our regular chores. As I milked, the warmth from the cow's big stolid body was comforting in the nippy late evening air. I sat close to her on my three-legged stool, and my experienced hands sent the streams of milk pinging against the side and bottom of my bucket.

"Meow, Meow!" There was Mother Cat rubbing against me, serving notice that she wanted her supper. In her cat way she knew that we were milking. As soon as she had my attention, she stood on her hind legs close by, and I expertly squirted streams of the fresh warm milk onto her little pink tongue and she, just as expertly, lapped it into her mouth. As was not uncommon with us, I began talking to her, "You need extra milk so you can have plenty for your baby kittens. We found your nest in the haymow where you hid it, but you mustn't know that we discovered it, for we don't want you to move your babies."

By the time I had stripped my cows dry, my bucket was full of white frothy liquid, and I called to Mother Cat, "Come on to the house with me and I'll give you some more milk."

She followed closely at my heels from the barn and into the yard. Up on the slop bucket bench she jumped and waited patiently until I had skimmed the foam from the top of my milk pail and into her eating pan. This was the regular diet given to our cat family, and by this time Old Tom had joined her, making sure he would get his share.

Gradually winter weather crept over our farm as the grass turned dry and anemic. The maple trees in the front yard defrocked and went to sleep. The fields now stripped of their crops lay barren around the farm buildings. Old Tom and Mother Cat slipped into the house at every opportunity and slept behind the kitchen stove. We no longer took the cows to the back pasture, but they remained in the barn yard where they huddled together against the straw rick or in the slanting rays of the winter sun. The cold crept into our house around the windows and under the doors, and Mother pushed pairs of the men's worn trousers against the bottoms of the doors to keep the warmth in and the cold out. The frost on the window panes froze, forming beautiful patterns, flowers, ferns and tall grasses. The moisture condensed on our walls and trickled down in little rivulets. At night we were reluctant to go to bed in our unheated upstairs rooms, and when finally human generators warmed our beds to a comfortable temperature, we snuggled down and slept on undisturbed, ignoring the cold around us. Each morning, shrouded in our longwear, we dashed down stairs to dress in the warmth of the front room stove in which Pappy had earlier kindled a fire.

Then the snows came. They silently blanketed the fields, the hills, the mountains surrounding us. The landscape was chaste and unsullied, no grime from a polluted world. Our path in the snow crisscrossed from house to barn, to chicken house, to the corn crib, as we performed our daily chores.

We children welcomed the snow; we still made opportunities to go coasting with our neighborhood friends. For the first time the

Pence family had a store-bought sled instead of depending entirely on homemade ones—Bertha had bought a "Flexible Flyer." It was ecstasy to fly down the hills on this sleek lightweight coaster with its smooth iron runners. No modern day toboggan or skis ever provided more delight to a family of children unaccustomed to the thrills of our present age! Imagine, if you will, walking a mile or two in the cold and snow to our appointed meeting place with our friends, pulling sleds up the steep hill, taking turns in riding down again, afterwards trudging home through the dark and cold, then to bed. Is it any wonder that we needed no pills, Nytol or Sominex, to put us to sleep?

We celebrated Christmas with the same simplicity that our family had in times past—but this year Pappy purchased a whole bushel of oranges, and as long as they lasted everyone had a treat of an orange while we sat around the heating stove at night before bedtime. Without knowing it, we had an abundance of what modern psychologists choose to call "family togetherness."

We still enjoyed the Christmas custom of gathering up old clothes and a sugar poke or lisle stocking mask, donning them, then driving off in the frozen night air to go belsnickeling. Also groups of belsnicklers continued to call at our house throughout the holidays.

One snowy day, while Pappy was relaxing in his special chair by the stove, he spied partridges waddling along the boxwood and fence in the front yard searching for food.

"The partridges are having a hard time since they can't go to the ground to find food with all this snow. Jake, go to the barn and bring in some wheat to scatter around out there for them." Pappy knew that such birds were valuable assets to a farm and he felt called to protect them.

Each day thereafter, Jake would scatter a portion of grain to help them through the winter, until springtime came again and the snows were gone.

January and February came and went; March followed with its weather behaving rather capriciously. Then suddenly it was April! We had weathered another winter!

Spring is the time of new beginnings—never more apparent than on a farm. In the creeks, the fields, the orchards, the garden, the barnyard, life that had lain dormant all winter was now exploding around us.

Young active bodies that had been shrouded in long underwear and heavy black stockings many months, longing to be free, now flexed and expanded breaking out of their cocoons.

Just as surely as life changes from season to season and chores on a farm adjust to these changes, so, too, the lives of families and each individual member also undergo metamorphoses. Each one grows and develops and matures; for each there are endings and new beginnings. These transitions, too, sometimes pass tranquilly and almost unnoticed, until an event, a happening, an encounter occurs, and one suddenly realizes that things aren't the same as they once were. Friends are no longer the spindly-legged flat-chested little girls they used to be. Local boys seemed to be undergoing a transformation too; they appeared less gawky and awkward and occasionally their behavior seemed almost human.

Then Elizabeth B. had a date with one! Gee whiz! What was happening to us? We thought and talked about our futures still—about finishing high school—perhaps college—what we really wanted to be when we were grown.

I still had my dreams and aspirations, but they took on a more mature and practical aspect now, not so much fantasizing in an unreal world.

As I looked at myself in our same diffused bespeckled mirror, I was not unhappy with the image reflected there—my eyes, hair, eyebrows, my slightly up-tilted nose, my square jaws were a part of my personality, my character, they were "me." I was not exactly beautiful, but neither did I think I was ugly. I certainly was no Mary Pickford. Did I want to be?

As for transforming myself into a Pollyanna and pretending to be glad all the time, I realized that wasn't "me" either, and never would be. I didn't always have to be glad, sometimes I could be sad, happy, angry, good or bad. No one knew that better than Mother and Pappy.

Then there was that once upon a time missionary appeal to my youthful vulnerable emotions. By now it was becoming apparent that self-denial was not my number one virtue, and I was not ready to give my life completely to the church. There was much fun and joy and carefreeness I wanted to yet experience in my young life. I didn't know if I would ever be good or wise enough to be a missionary like David Livingstone.

I still loved to read romances and identify with the characters and often dream of what the future might bring. Maybe someday my knight in shining armor would come—he probably would be no Ramon Navarro, nor Rudolph Valentino, or even a Pollyanna orphan boy adopted by a wealthy man.

Once Mother had said, "Esther is very stubborn and determined. She'll probably be whatever she wants to be."

I didn't know if this was or was not a compliment. But I did know that in the years that lay ahead, whatever opportunities and challenges might inspire or intrigue or beckon, I could always be "me"!

Date Due

10-2			
12/4			

BRODART, INC. Cat. No. 23 233 Printed in U.S.A.